DIAMOND AND THE

TALENT SHOW

DIAMOND AND THE TALENT SHOW

Ruth McGhee

Avarnia Publishing House

Text copyright 2021 by Avarnia Publishing House

Cover photograph copyright 2021 by Avarnia Publishing House

Library of Congress Cataloging-In-Publication Data is available upon request.

ISBN

Printed in the United States of America

To the trail blazers who paved the way for me: Bernice Brown and Ruthie McGhee.

To my foundation: Nancy Zanders Green (Hiney), Sheilda Brown, Patricia McGhee

& my mom, dad, siblings (AG, Nia, Belle, and Dre)…I love you!

Thank you for always supporting me 😊

-Ruby

"Life is not measured by the number of breaths you take, but by the moments that take your breath away."

— **Maya Angelou**

"If there is a book that you want to read, but it hasn't been written yet, you must be the one to write it."

—**Toni Morrison**

"A crown, if it hurts us, is not worth wearing."

— **Pearl Bailey**

Contents

Chapter 1

TALENT SHOW

"Quiet. Shh…Silence!", she spat, her glasses sliding down her nose from the effort. "Listen to the morning announcement silently or complete silent independent work for the rest of class."

My teacher Mrs. Johnson - AKA Mrs. Meanie - said with a glare. 'Silent' is her favorite word, by far. I'm pretty sure it makes up about 50% of her daily vocabulary usage. The word "detention" comes at a close second. If she had her way, there would be no noise at all in the world. As the class quieted down to listen to the morning announcement, a muffled sound and a blurry image appeared on our Smart Board. Mrs. Meanie is dreadful at working with technology. If you squinted, you could vaguely see two teachers holding identical cups of coffee, brandishing large smiles. They spoke with slightly forced cheery voices. One of them was holding a bright neon poster with a large word that started with the letter "T".

One of the teachers began talking. "I am so excited to announce that our annual talent show is now set to begin!" she exclaimed clapping her hands together. "Registration forms will be accepted starting today. Talents can be anything from singing, dancing, playing an instrument, doing magic tricks, or any other cool school-appropriate activity that you would like to showcase to your fellow classmates. If you are confused about whether your talent is school-appropriate or not, ask your teacher! The grand prize will be announced in a week."

A burst of chatter filled the room that even Mrs. Meanie couldn't control. Her face flushed as the room filled with laughter, ideas and jokes.

"Silence! I see you've made your decision. You will do silent independent work for the rest of the class. Take out a pencil and paper. It's math time." The class groaned as Mrs. Meanie simply smiled as if all her dreams had come true in that very moment.

As we started to settle down and start our independent work, Kiara quietly slipped me a note that read, "The winners, by a landslide, of the annual Jackson Middle School talent show are Kiara and Diamond, with their amazing flute and saxophone duet." I tried to suppress a laugh that ended in a loud snort, earning me a glare from Mrs. Meanie.

The minutes in the class seemed to last hours, but an eternity later the bell rang, and the class finally ended. "Make sure to do your homework! It's due tomorrow!" Mrs. Meanie shouted after us, as everyone tried to leave as quickly as possible.

"What song do you want to play?" I asked Kiara as we left the classroom.

"I dunno." She replied, a little distracted.

"Well, it's gotta be hard…...but not too hard. It's gotta be popular, but school appropriate. Plus, we need to have it ready in a month." I said as I ticked off the points on my fingers.

"Yeah," she agreed, doing the sort of slow nod with her head that people usually do when they're pretending to listen to someone. Her eyes were locked to something in the distance. "Hey, have you seen this poster?" she asked, pointing to the wall across from us.

I looked forward and saw a poster, with big neon green font that read, "Join Maggie's Band for the talent show! Tryouts at my house. See me for address and details." Followed by a bunch of annoying hearts she likes to draw next to everything.

"I thought she's said bands are lame!" I exclaimed in disbelief.

"Yeah!" Kiara agreed, frowning. "Does she even play an instrument?!"

Before we had time to process Maggie's poster, the bell rang, reminding us that we had to get to class. "Oh shoot! I'm going be late for Home Ec! Bye!" I exclaimed, running off.

Home Ec that day was rather unusual. We were instructed to follow a recipe on the board and make biscuits, but nearly everyone burned their batches because we were distracted by conversations about the talent show. People had a lot of ideas... Some were idiotic and would never be approved by the school, while others had pretty good potential. I took my notebook out and wrote down some of the ideas I heard:

- Burping the alphabet
- Reciting the numbers of pi (yawn)
- Singing
- Dancing
- Jumping rope
- Rapping
- Acting
- Modeling (oh boy)
- Styling hair on a mannequin
- Dribbling a basketball to the beat of a song (I'd like to see *that* happen)
- Doing push ups
- Making a peanut butter and jam sandwich (I wish I was joking)
- Cleaning up a mess in record time with an invention

4

The rest were band ideas in duets or trios.

Almost everyone that played an instrument or sang was talking about joining Maggie's Band. I had to stop myself from rolling my eyes – I mean, the girl only had one poster up! They were all certain she was going to win too and wanted to be a part of the winning team.

When the bell chimed to end class, to go to lunch, I wasn't in the best of moods. I definitely didn't want to hear anything else about Maggie's stupid band anymore. But as I turned the corner to head to lunch, I was nearly blinded by a new wave of neon pink font and hearts. I didn't know whether to puke or scream.

"Okay, Diamond. You're overreacting. What's so bad about a few posters?" you might ask. Allow me to explain.

This wasn't just a few posters – this was a hallway *filled* with them. It was as if someone had barfed up glitter, hearts, and neon colors all over the hallway walls. Everywhere you went, you saw a poster inviting you to join Maggie's Band followed by the utterly stupid hearts she draws next to everything. *Is this even allowed?* I said to myself as I tried to walk away as fast as I could without bumping into other students to escape the horror.

I noticed a teacher walk into that very hallway as I was heading out. She was busy on her phone so she initially didn't notice the posters. It was until she was in the middle of the hallway that she abruptly stopped and looked around with a gasp. I waited for her to form a scowl and go straight to the principal and inform her that the posters are a major threat to the public's eyes and that the sight of them might induce vomiting and seizures. Instead, she shook her head in awe and exclaimed to the students around her, "The creativity of these students is amazing! These are some brilliantly made posters, aren't they?". She looked around some more and continued as she was.

It took every ounce in me to prevent my jaw from hitting the ground. I hurried off to my locker to get my lunch. *Isn't there some famous saying that everything looks better after lunch?* I was sure hoping that was true.

When I entered the lunchroom, I started looking for Kiara but instead, I saw utter chaos. Maggie was surrounded by nearly the entire Jackson Middle School Band, Orchestra and Chorus. I walked over to hear Maggie say, "Yes, anyone is welcome for tryouts...if you're not a nerd of course. So that means...you, you, you, you, you, you, and you." As she was going around the mob around her, she turned to a group of shy, band students and said, "Your little group should just save their time and leave," and continued to scan the rest of the group in the same way.

Why do people like her? I thought to myself, struck with horror.

A boy I didn't know raised his hand as if Maggie was a teacher and he was a student and said, "What makes your band better than other bands? You've got a lot of competition with other student bands signing up for the Talent Show."

Maggie just laughed, smiled, and seemed to look directly at me and said, "Yeah, that's not a question we're even thinking about. We're going to win. If you make the cut for my band, it's a guaranteed first place."

I shook my head and went to find the table Kiara was sitting at. Kiara was sitting at our usual table eating the school food with disgust painted all over her face. I sat down next to her and told her what I heard Maggie say. Kiara rolled her eyes. "That girl's ego is bigger than an Amphicoelous."

I raised an eyebrow at her in confusion.

"It's a dinosaur. My little brothers are obsessed with them right now", she replied.

I laughed. Kiara has a way of making random connections. As we finished up our lunch, I said to her, "We *have* to win now – against all odds."

Kiara agreed. "Diamond, can you cover me?"

"Sure," I said.

"Cover me" is code for "I'm going to use my phone. Make sure I don't get caught." The risk of getting caught is high and the punishment a guaranteed lunch detention the next day. Kiara skillfully whipped out her phone and quickly put it under the table. With quick typing skills, she began searching the web... for whatever she was searching for.

I began to scan the lunchroom. A teacher locked eyes with me. *What should I do to not look guilty?!* I thought. I quickly looked away while simultaneously trying not to lose her in the lunchroom, which is a pretty difficult feat. The teacher's eyebrows immediately raised at my suspicious squirming and not-so-great covering. *Uh-oh.* "Teacher, Kiara." I whispered.

"I nearly have it though!" Kiara said quickly, scrolling through her phone.

"She's walking over. Turn it off!" I say, rushed.

"One more minute! Stall her or something!" Kiara exclaimed.

"This isn't like in the movies! Turn it off!" I whispered hurriedly.

"Stall her, please!" Kiara muttered focused entirely on her phone.

"Kiara, this better be important." I whispered back annoyed. I stood up and walked over to the teacher. "Hello, I was... Um..." I started fiddling with my hands. "I'm wondering if, um... I'm wondering what's for lunch tomorrow?" I asked nervously, a small awkward laugh escaping my mouth.

"It's Nacho Tuesday," she replied, stopping to give me a second of her attention only to walk briskly toward Kiara again.

"Wait!" I exclaimed. The teacher stopped and frowned at me. "I...um...have another question," I said while my mind went into panic mode. I'm not the best around authority figures. The teacher nodded for me to continue. "Ummm...I was wondering if you knew when the...oh, lacrosse team forms are due!"

The teacher frowned sympathetically as she said, "Oh I'm sorry honey. The lacrosse forms were due last week."

I did my best to look disappointed even though I couldn't care less about lacrosse. I'm more of a tennis girl anyways. She smiled sweetly at me and then continued to walk briskly toward Kiara, just as Kiara slipped her phone back into her pocket. The teacher gave her a hard look, finding no evidence of wrongdoing, and walked away to bust another kid. I slowly walked back to the table relieved and angry.

"That better be important," I groaned, sitting back into my seat.

She smiled and said, "I know what song we're gonna play."

"What?" I asked, getting excited.

"Against all odds by peace man." Kiara said excitedly.

Peace man is a hippie rapper, who doesn't curse, promote violence, or say anything inappropriate. He wears tie-dye shirts in all his music videos, and ends all of them by throwing a peace sign up at the camera. Not only is he school-appropriate, but the teachers will probably love him. Who doesn't?

I smiled. "It's perfect."

"I know," she said smugly. "But let's stop talking about the talent show. I've been hearing about it-"

"All day? Yeah, me too. I'll change the subject. How was your soccer game?" I asked ready, to hear a blow-by-blow detail of a game I cared nothing about.

Kiara did not disappoint. She went on about the "awful" referee, the missed penalty kick that cost her team the game, and something about her coach sitting her down in "clutch time" even though she wasn't even that tired. Soccer is Kiara's world. She's known to have run on broken legs during soccer games, claiming she was feeling refreshed. After she was done ranting, it was my turn to tell her all about my tennis match, as she faked excitement and anger at all the right parts.

The lunch bell rang, and we went on our way to class. After every lunch talk (or rant) with Kiara, I always feel good. Even thousands of "Maggie's Band" posters, snide remarks and silent classes couldn't take away that feeling. As I walked to band class, I saw the talent show sign-up sheets hanging on the bulletin board. There were five of them, pinned in one long row, all full to the brim with weird names like Billy, Bob, and John Cena. The names were either written next to "magic act" or "Maggie's Band".

As I approached the board to get a closer view of the sheets, I saw a big, yellow banner pinned above the sheets that read, "FULL. No longer taking applications." The words were written with what seemed to be a glittery silver colored marker. What was strange was that the words were followed by a heart...A very familiar heart at that.

My heart dropped at the sight of this.

Chapter 2

TROUBLE

I walked to the band room devastated and played my flute with no enthusiasm at all. The rest of the day felt like a very long pity party. There was a lot of excited talent show talk going on around me but all it did was remind me that I couldn't be a part of the show with Kiara.

As I got on the bus, I found a seat close to the front so I could properly sulk by myself. However, the moment was not very long lived, as two minutes later my friend Amelia plopped down next to me, sputtering her words so fast they were barely audible.

"I just can't wait to do the talent show!" She exclaimed, swaying side to side excitedly. "I'm going to sing. I just need to find out what song I'm going to do. What are you doing for the talent show?" She asked looking at me expectantly.

Even though me and Amelia were good friends, in that moment I wanted to slap her and hide away from the world.

"Nothing," I mumbled, hoping she could catch a hint as I turned to glance out the window.

"Huh, well, why not?!" she asked sympathetically.

The anger inside me started to build, despite my rational side's constant reminders that she meant the best. "The talent form sheet is full. No more applications are being accepted." I said through tightly clenched teeth. "You probably signed up this morning, right?"

There was a pause. "N-nooo, I didn't" Amelia said looking as if she had seen a ghost.

I instantly felt better, and then I wanted to slap myself for feeling happy about it.

"I thought it didn't matter how many people sign up." Amelia continued. "They usually let everyone sign up and hold a round of auditions before the actual talent show to kick out the worst, until there's a reasonable amount of people." Amelia murmured each word laced in worry.

"Well, I guess not this year," I sighed looking at the window gloomily but stopped as the sun reigned war on my eyes. How is anyone supposed to properly sulk if rain doesn't hit the window that they're looking out of, like in the movies?

"You know what, they probably made a mistake. That's how they always run the talent show. Why would they change it this year?" Amelia asked, talking more to herself than to me. "I'm going to email the teacher in charge. We at least deserve a shot. How in the world did the sign-up sheet fill up that quickly in a day anyway? I mean that's unheard of! Did you see any of the names on the list?" Amelia asked.

"Look Amelia, maybe it just wasn't meant to be."

"I don't believe that." Amelia said, whipping out her phone. "Who runs the talent show?"

"Mrs. Donlon," I sighed. Amelia was going through all types of stages of grief. I guess I had hit acceptance by that point, and she was still staggering in anger and denial.

She punched in some numbers in her phone. It rang three times and a person on the other side picked up. In the sweetest voice that kids use toward adults when they want something, Amelia said "Hello, may I talk to Mrs. Donlon? …Thank you." She said, and paused to wait for Mrs. Donlon to come to the phone.

"You *called* her?" I mouthed. "Why didn't you just email?"

She mouthed something back but all I read was, "Ice Komodo pony" so I just waited for her to continue the phone conversation.

"Hello, yes, I have a question about the talent show. There was a yellow banner that said no more applications were being accepted. Is that true?" There was a lengthy pause. "Thank you for the clarification. Have a nice day! Bye." She hung up the phone quickly and smiled at me. "I was right!" She exclaimed triumphantly.

"Wait, what?" I asked, momentarily pausing my sulking.

"It must have been some big mistake or something. She said she's been getting emails all day about it. She checked the sign-up sheets, and she noticed a lot of fake names after the few real sign-ups." She said excitedly. "A student wrote "FULL" message so other people wouldn't sign up! She said when she finds out who did it, they'll get two weeks of lunch detention and will not be able to participate in the talent show." She paused to take a breath.

"Did you recognize the handwriting?" Amelia then asked.

"No..." but then it clicked. "Amelia! I remember. The written message was followed by a heart! The very same heart that Maggie draws next to everything! Plus, Maggie's band was on the list! She had to have done it!"

"I think you're right." Amelia said, nodding slowly. "Should we tell someone?" She asked, looking towards me.

I shrugged. "It's not like we have any evidence. Anyway, her punishment will be one of us beating her to the prize!"

"You got that right!" Amelia said laughing.

All the while Amelia and I were chatting away, there was a girl sitting behind us. When I quickly glanced to see who it was, I locked eyes with her - I recognized her as Maggie's best friend. She gasped as if caught in the act of eavesdropping on us, and turned her body towards the window as she pulled out her phone and started texting.

My phone buzzed and I saw I had gotten a text from Amelia. I guess she didn't want to be caught talking out loud.

Amelia: You think she heard that?

Diamond: Definitely.

Amelia: Then you know Maggie's is going to know soon. Right?

Diamond: What can she do? She's the one in hot water.

Amelia: I don't know. One of her talents is making herself the victim.

Diamond: You give her too much credit. She's the one that made that banner, not us. How could we get in trouble?

Amelia: You're probably right.

As the bus slowed to a rest at our stop, which happened to be the last, we got off, said our goodbyes to each other and walked to our houses. Thank goodness the school day was finally over.

I walked towards my family's stand-alone, gated house with a big, patchy front yard. I passed the rusty grill was typically always placed underneath the big tree to the left of the yard and went straight inside.

You could describe the inside of my house as...quite lived-in. You will always find an occasional tennis racket, or basketball, on the floor of the entrance hallway. Occasional homework packets are left sprawled on the table and essentially any counter-space. I walked over the mess of shoes by the door and headed upstairs, into my bedroom, one of the messiest rooms in the house by far. I never make the bed, so the covers are left disheveled all day and night. My closet is a constant mess with clothes falling off half-broken hangers, while a few clothes can be seen lying on the floor where I can easily spot them, and so on.

I quickly got dressed into a comfier outfit and headed to the kitchen to grab a bite. I share the house with 5 other siblings – 3 brothers and 2 sisters – so snacks are not a problem to find. Brayton is my oldest sibling and likes to feel in charge since he's in grade 10. He plays football and soccer. I'm the next in line. I'm in grade 7 and play tennis and track. Deliah is younger than me and is the family's official tattletale. If you do something around her, our parents are sure to know about it. She is in grade 2, along with my other sister, Diana, who is starting her first season of soccer. Being twins, they are inseparable. Benjamin, or Ben, is only 4 years old and likes to take advantage of the rest of his siblings to get what he wants, though he usually picks Diana and Blake to annoy. Blake is two years old, and he is thriving in his terrible twos. And that's my loud, sporty family. If we're not driving each other crazy in the house, we're going to sport practices and meets.

Anyways, as I walked into the living room, Ben and Blake were there to meet me along with my mom. Since middle schoolers came home first, high schoolers second and elementary school students last, I naturally was always the first home.

"Hi, Diamond!" Benjamin said excitedly. Blake sucked on his lollipop.

"Hi Benjamin! Hi, Blake! Hi, Mom. How was work?" I asked.

My mom groaned. "Work was work. How was school?" My Mom replied.

"Good," I said heading out of the mudroom. "I'm entering the talent show."

"Nice. Are you doing an act with Kiara?" My Mom replied as she headed upstairs.

"Yes," I replied as I followed her upstairs while Benjamin and Blake trailed behind me, snacking on some cookies as Ben and Blake trailed after me. While my mom went to her bedroom, I went back into mine and started to do some homework before I procrastination hit. I decided to get started on English homework when my phone rang. I answered it to hear the worried voice of Kiara.

"Did you hear that no more talent show applications are being accepted?' Kiara asked to start the conversation.

"Yeah…" I said.

"Can you believe that? How can it fill up that quickly anyway? I emailed Mrs. Donlon for clarification but she hasn't responded yet! It's probably true. It's sad that we can't even have a chance to do the talent show!" She said in an angry jumble.

"It's not true," I said quickly before she could start another rant.

"What? How do you know?" She asked.

"Amelia called Mrs. Donlon and found out that a teacher didn't make the banner that said no more applications were being accepted..."

"Huh? Then who did?" She asked cutting me off.

"The talent show is running how it did last year. A student did it to stop other people from signing up. *I think* Maggie did it to eliminate the competition." I said with confidence. I heard a gasp on the other side.

"Maggie did it!? Do you know that for sure?" She asked.

"Well, the "FULL" message was followed by a heart and her name was on the list..." I explained.

"That's not solid proof." Kiara said brushing it off, disappointed. "Look, I have to go. I haven't started my science project yet and its due tomorrow. My mom's gonna kill me if she sees another "C" on my report card." Kiara said while sighing.

"Okay. But I know Maggie did it!."

"*Okay, okay*. Bye." Kiara said.

I ended the call at the same time I heard our front door open. I sighed as I realized my peaceful moment at the house was officially gone for the day.

"Hi, Mom!" Brayton hollered, bounding up the steps. His bedroom door slammed and music began pounding down the hallways and vibrating through the walls. I tried to ignore the music and resume my homework but all you heard was a rapid beat and words being rapped so fast I couldn't make a single word out."

"Turn it down Brayton!" I hollered, entering the hallway to pound my fist on his door.

"Fine!" He hollered back. The noise died down for roughly 0.05 seconds and was back to the same, rowdy volume by the time I returned to my room.

The Next Day

"Blake, please eat your oatmeal…Deliah and Diana, time to come down for breakfast...Have a good day at school Diamond…Oh, Brayton, you almost forgot your lunch." My mom informed to us five siblings as she got her papers ready for her job. Brayton rushed out the door to his bus stop as Blake poked at his oatmeal.

"Thanks mom!" I said as I headed out the door with my dad. He drove me to the bus stop, wished me a good day and dropped me off so he could get ready for work as well. As I waited for the bus stop, Amelia got dropped off by her parents and we talked about the last episode of "Me and My Crazy Life" starring myself, until the bus pulled up.

Amelia and I sat towards the end of the bus and talked the entire ride to school. When we arrived at school, we parted ways and went to our 1rst period classes. There, Mrs. Meanie overused the word "silence" as usual and put on the morning announcements that was as blurry as yesterday's. This time, however, there were no forced smiles and bright posters. Only two grim faces with their identical cups of coffee. "Good morning students," the teacher on the right said. "As some of you may have seen, yesterday there was a yellow banner on the talent show sign-up sheet that said "No more applications were being accepted"."

The teacher on the left continued, "However, that is not true. A student made that banner and filled the sign-up sheets with fake names to make the appearance that it was full." She took a deep breath and gave a hard look at the camera as if scanning the entire school's faces to find who was guilty.

I glanced at Maggie. She had on the best poker face I've ever seen. "Once, we find out who did this," she took a brief pause and cast a look that would turn Medusa into stone, "the punishment will be severe."

The teacher on the right nodded and continued, "Yes, it will be. Two weeks of lunch detention and absolutely no participation in the talent show."

The room suddenly felt colder. I looked at Maggie and noticed her face went a bit pale. "But if the student comes forward, the punishment will only be 1 week of lunch detention and still no participation in the talent show." She smiled warmly as she said that statement as if it was that much better.

The teacher on the left nodded. "We also highly encourage anyone with information to come forward. If you saw who did it, or heard someone bragging about doing this, you know where to find us." She gave a slight smile.

The teacher on the right nodded once again. "You can also email us and ask to be kept anonymous. Students who have been suspected by a letter or email will be asked to report to the principal's office for further questioning starting today. This is not something to play around with. If you have any further questions about this issue, please contact us in email or in person."

I droned out the rest of the morning announcements wondering if I should write a letter, but I knew I had no solid evidence – just speculation and pure bias towards Maggie.

Maggie's face lit up once the announcements were done and whipped out a sparkly glitter pen. She then began to write what looked like a letter titled, "Yellow Banner." *Was she giving herself up? That didn't seem like Maggie,* I thought to myself.

Mrs. Meanie, on the other hand, had formed a frown on her face and had her hand on her hip. "This is a very important problem, so I want those of you who know anything about the matter to write your letters now, so it can be addressed as soon as possible. If you did not see anyone put the banner up, work on the worksheets I will hand out momentarily." At that moment I wished I had seen Maggie do it. Throughout the period, everybody but Maggie worked on the math worksheets. She was taking her sweet time writing away. I was enjoying the thought of her apologizing a million times and begging for her spot back in the talent show. Before I could indulge in that thought any longer, she took her letter up to Mrs. Meanie with an innocent smile and a skip in her step.

I was starting to think that maybe the truth had set her free, and she's not as bad as I thought she was.

Finally, 1rst period ended and I was off to Phys Ed with Amelia. However, as our gym teacher was explaining the rules to volleyball, a loud screech went over the intercom. "Can Amelia Anderson and Diamond Smith report to the principal's office?" A breathy voice said with a pause, **"…immediately."**

You could hear the sneer in her voice. Ooh's broke out around the room. I cast a worried glance at Amelia feeling the burning and accusing eyes of my classmates on me. Our gym teacher dismissed us and walked slowly out the gym room, feeling humiliated.

As soon as we got out of eye's reach outside of the gym, I exhaled. "Amelia, they think we did it!" I exclaimed with defeat. "We're going to get kicked out of the show for something we didn't do!" I gasped, "My mom will be so furious!"

"Calm down," Amelia said looking the opposite of calm. "They don't have any proof and we're innocent until proven guilty. Besides, we're completely assuming that this has to do with the yellow banner. Let's be on our way and see what this is all about."

A few minutes later, we had arrived at the principal's office. We walked in with our heads hanging low as the principal greeted us with a blank expression.

"Hello ladies," she said, casting a stern look.

"Hello, Mrs. Baxter," me and Amelia chanted. We sat down on the chairs lined up across her desk.

"We'll start our meeting after the last guest has arrived," she said. Like clockwork, in walked Kiara. My jaw dropped as I saw her, and her jaw dropped as she saw me.

Once the door was shut and Kiara was seated, Mrs. Baxter continued, "By now you may be guessing this has to do with the yellow banner. If you fess up to your actions now, the punishment will still be less severe," she offered.

"Mrs. Baxter, we didn't do it," Amelia said. Mrs. Baxter studied us sternly.

"We take these types of matters very seriously. If you have anything to do with messing with the sign-up sheets, please speak up now." We all shook our heads in unison. "Very well then. I will conduct a locker search today as soon as I notify your parents. If they respond quickly, this process should only take about 10 minutes. The offer to confess still stands." Then she turned to her computer and sent three identical emails to our parents. We sat in awkward, nervous silence glancing at each other. We knew she wouldn't find anything in our lockers, but the entire process was still nerve wracking.

Three chimes came in about five minutes later. She checked her emails, gave a brief nod, and said, "Follow me." Her bright red high heels clacked on the floor, and we all followed her nervously. The hallway seemed to stretch on forever. We finally stopped at Amelia's locker and Mrs. Baxter asked her to open it. It took multiple tries to open it and a lot of tugging but with a final groan and a heave, Amelia's locker opened. Yellow banner paper and glittery colored markers came tumbling out. My jaw dropped and my hand flew to my mouth. Amelia looked just as surprised as me to see the stuff in her locker.

"It wasn't me Mrs. Baxter. I don't know how that got in there. I-I-I promise!" she said desperately. Mrs. Baxter cast a sad look towards her and shook her head slowly. You could see tears forming in Amelia's eyes.

"I wish I could believe you, Amelia. But this evidence, along with the fact that a student claimed to see you make the banner and hang it up, suggests elsewise."

Then, Mrs. Baxter walked on with the sickening clack of her heels against the tile floor. I glanced at Amelia. I've known Amelia since the 5th grade. She was the most trustful, rule-abiding person I know. Had she really made the banner? Amelia walked on slowly, sniffling, as tears rolled down her cheeks. I had never seen Amelia cry before, and I felt bad. But the evidence was not in her favor, and I wasn't sure if she did it or not. I glanced at her, but she turned away. In shame or in anger I did not know.

We stopped at Kiara's locker next. I glanced at her face, and she seemed relaxed and confident. With a mighty pull on the lock, her locker opened and the same yellow banner paper and glittery markers that were in Amelia's locker tumbled out on the floor, falling at Mrs. Baxter's feet. Shock was coming over me, as I started to realize that maybe the two friends I trusted the most might have made the yellow banner. I looked at Kiara. She looked as if she had seen a ghost. "Mrs. Baxter, I honestly don't know where this came from!" she exclaimed.

"I'm sorry, Kiara, but I the evidence speaks for itself." Mrs. Baxter sighed. "Diamond, is there anything you'd like to say before I check your locker?"

I shook my head. She let out a little sigh, turned on her heel and started the horrible clacking of her heels toward my locker. With each step she took, I felt like I was going to throw up. When we arrived, she asked me to open my locker. I had held my breath until I saw that no yellow banner or glittery markers fell out. A big wave of relief washed over me. She started shifting my locker contents around to make sure she left no stone unturned, while I could see a look of confusion on her face grow. Finally, she looked in the last corner of my locker and pulled out neatly folded, wonderfully hidden, yellow banner paper and a couple of glittery colored markers. I was at a loss for words. My knees buckled and my breath came out fast. "B--b-b-but I-I-I-I-I didn't do it!" I exclaimed. "I promise!"

She gave me the same slow shake of the head she gave Amelia and Kiara. "I am so sorry girls. I want to believe you, but this is sadly enough evidence suggesting you each had a part in messing with the talent show. You girls *do* however seem so sincere and have such good behavioral records that if you prove you didn't do it within a week, you will not be punished." We all let out an identical sigh of relief. "However," she said sharply, "I *will* have to notify your parents."

And with that, I was as good as dead.

Chapter 3

FACING MY FAMILY

I walked back home after school ended, knowing quite well that I wouldn't return. "Diamond Grace Smith get upstairs now!" my mother seethed as soon as I walked through the door.

"Yes ma'am," I replied meekly as I flung off my shoes, shrugged off my jacket and ran upstairs to my room where she was waiting for me at the foot of my bed. "Angry" couldn't describe her face. She was furious, seething, enraged, and irate combined into one expression.

"I got a call from your principal today." She said while Benjamin and Blake peeked their heads into my room to listen to in on the conversation. I raised my eyebrows in surprise, trying to play dumb. "Why did you create a banner that said no more applications were being accepted? For a…" she flung her hands up in the air, "stupid talent show?"

I cringed under the anger and embarrassment. I normally didn't get in trouble, so this really hurt. "Mom, I-I" I hesitated under her glare, "didn't do it," I said quietly.

"Diamond! Are you really going to lie to my face?" she exclaimed, as if debating whether to kill me on the spot or not. "The principal said she found identical yellow banner paper and colored glittery markers in your locker! Very well hidden, too! I didn't even buy you glittery colored markers! Where did they come from?"

I shook my head, "Mom, I have no idea. I promise it wasn't me! Someone must've put the stuff in my locker."

"Really, Diamond? Someone put the stuff in your locker!" My mom yelled, her voice climbing higher and higher. "Give me your electronics! I'm going to have to discuss this with your father." I defeatedly gave her my phone and flopped on my bed as soon as she left my room. I sat and I looked in the mirror. A tear slid down my cheek.

30 minutes later, Brayton came home. By then I had calmed down a bit. Downstairs, I heard Mom ask about Brayton's day with an unusual coolness. She was definitely still angry. I heard the creaking of the steps as Brayton made his way upstairs. Then, I heard the creaking of my door as it opened. "What's made mom so angry? Wait, are you crying?" he asked as he studied my face. I wiped my gross, runny nose on my sleeve.

"No reason. Don't you have stuff to do?"

"What you did is what I want to know!" Brayton said, slinging his backpack on the floor as he made himself comfortable at my desk. "Miss goody two shoes finally got in trouble? I need the story." I rolled my eyes.

"It's that stupid talent show." I said, sighing. "A student made a banner that misled students into believing there were no more applications being accepted even though there was tons of room left. And everyone thinks I did it, including mom." My face got hot and I willed myself not to cry again.

"Well, why do they think you did it?"

"They think that Kiara, Amelia and I did it!"

"Isn't Amelia the girl that never got anything but an "A" in her life? And isn't Kiara the girl that's phenomenal at sports and got her first "C" ever last quarter, in advanced Algebra? She showed up some guys in basketball at your birthday party, right?" I nodded. "Why in the world do they think you guys did it? You guys are such rule-abiding students, " he said, throwing up his hands.

I smiled, deciding to take it as a compliment. "Well, they think it's us because someone turned in an anonymous note saying that he or she saw us doing it."

"Well, that's not really proof."

"And...they did a locker search. They found the identical yellow banner paper and matching glittery markers in all of our lockers," I said, looking at the ground. He raised an eyebrow. He looked me straight in the eyes and studied me for about 10 seconds. I was just about to tell him to stop being weird when he said, "I believe you didn't do it. Even if all the evidence seems stacked against you."

I smiled. "Well, I'm glad someone believes me."

"Find a way to prove your innocence," he said as if it was as easy as strolling through a garden.

"How?" I asked, starting to get annoyed.

"I dunno. Talk to your friends, talk to other people, interrogate people, find out who wrote the anonymous note..." he said absentmindedly.

I froze. "Wait a minute! Say the last thing again!" I exclaimed.

He shrugged, "Interrogate people?".

"After that!" I exclaimed excitedly.

"I dunno."

"*Think*, Brayton. After that!" I was shivering with excitement.

"Find out who wrote the anonymous note?" he asked.

"Maggie." I spat.

"Huh?" Brayton asked.

"Uh, it's nothing," I muttered. "You know the story now. You can leave." I said dismissing him, completely in my own zone.

"Sure..." he said while leaving my room. As soon as he left, I sat down at my desk, my breathing speeding up. I sat at the foot of my bed seething, trying to think about a way to prove I didn't do it along with my friends and make sure that Maggie got in trouble. After an entire 30 minutes I came up completely empty.

Sighing, I decided to clear my mind and do some homework. I gloomily took out a pencil, a calculator, and a piece of scratch paper. After battling with my math equations for about 20 minutes, I heard the front door open downstairs.

"Hi, mom!" Deliah and Diana chanted. My mind went into a state of panic. Dad was home! He always picked up Deliah and Diana from school on the way home from work! I scurried around the room to find my thickest jeans, and my thickest sweater to prepare for a spanking. I mentally said goodbye to friend outings and texting, and I braced myself.

"Hi, honey," my dad said, most likely talking to my mom. I tip-toed to the very top of the steps to listen to the conversation.

"Hi," she said. Her voice was colder than the coldest day of winter. I cringed. *You're dead. You're dead. You're dead.* My brain chanted. "Diana and Deliah, can you go upstairs for a minute?"

I heard Diana and Deliah giggling as they headed upstairs. When they passed me on the stairs, they each gave me a sideways glance. Deliah frowned and looked at me with eyes full of mischief. "What are you doing?" she asked accusingly.

"Promise not to tell," I told her and stared at her hard.

She studied me weighing her options with her curiosity. "Fine," she sighed.

"I got in trouble at school and I'm spying to see how they're going to punish me," I said in a hurried jumble. "Now shush so I can listen."

"I want to spy too!" Diana exclaimed stamping her foot loudly.

I looked up in exasperation knowing if I denied her, she would just tell. "Fine," I said rolling my eyes. Diana and Deliah sat down next to me giggling. I put my finger to my mouth, and they slowly quieted down. By now my parents had already started the conversation.

"I got a call from Diamond's principal," my mom said.

"Oh, really. About what?" My dad asked in a bored tone.

"Diamond made some banner with her friends that said no more applications were being accepted for the talent show. Which is a lie. The evidence was found in her locker," my mom continued.

"What?" Dad asked. Deliah and Diana looked at me with wide eyes.

"I didn't do it!" I whispered aggressively. They clearly didn't believe me.

"Diamond, come downstairs," My dad called. I walked downstairs as if I was approaching a bomb about to go off. Which in a way, I was.

"Yes, dad?" I said, acting again as if I didn't know what was going on.

"Did you make the yellow banner that said no more applications were being accepted? And then lied to your mother about it repeatedly?" he asked.

"It's not a lie, I promise!" I said, urgently wondering what punishment lay in store for me.

My Dad sighed. Then my mom said, "Diamond, we 're going to give you a week to prove that you didn't make it."

I stood there. I wasn't going to get in trouble? My parents never do this!.

"You will be grounded until then and if you can't prove that it wasn't you within that time, then the punishment is going to be severe."

"Yes ma'am," I nodded nervously. I wasn't safe yet.

Chapter 4

THE TALK

After the talk with my parents, I walked upstairs into my room, deciphering what I was going to do while trying to remain calm. One week wasn't nearly long enough to prove my innocence and bust Maggie. It wasn't as if I just had all the time in the world to prove I was innocent either. Plus, I was grounded. *How am I supposed to do anything if I'm grounded,* I thought to myself. "Mission Impossible" had easier missions than this!

Besides, what were my friends going to do? No doubt they were getting in trouble too! *Gah, I hate Maggie! And I'm going to make her pay.* I paced back and forth but no ideas came to mind. That's the problem with the brain. In the moment of need, its efforts are very minimal in helping you find a solution. Then when the problem is already solved, suddenly you can think of ten different ways you could have handled the situation.

I flopped on my bed and took a deep breath. I was tired. I decided to think about something random, like why the sky is blue, instead of stressing out about the problem for another 30 minutes to give my mind a break.

***

The drive to my tennis practice the next day was unusually quiet, so much so that you could cut the tension with a giant, sharp-edged axe. When practice started, I wasn't performing well either – there was a lot on my mind.

Dinner that evening at the table was awkward and quiet as well. Everyone looked at me as if I had committed a murder. After dinner I went straight to bed at 9:30, which was a record, but I couldn't sleep. My thoughts tortured me and my mind played through the locker search repeatedly. I battled with my thoughts and tried to find some sort of peace. At about midnight, fatigue finally won but my sleep ended far too soon 7 hours later with a rough shake from my older brother.

"Wake up! You overslept. If you don't hurry, you're going to miss the bus." I turned to glance at the clock. 7:00 a.m. glared back at me. I jumped out of bed in a state of panic. My bus was going to come in five minutes. If I missed it, my mom would be furious. She might even change her mind about the week grace-period. I shivered just thinking about it.

I sprinted to the bathroom, brushed my teeth, raced downstairs, and impatiently waited for my dad to find his car keys. He drove us to the bus stop and we approached the bus just as it was about to leave. I jumped out of the car with my shoes untied, my hair an absolute disgrace, and my backpack falling off my shoulder. My stomach rumbled reminding me I hadn't eaten breakfast.

The bus stopped for us when the driver saw us running, and as I climbed aboard, she cast me an impatient glance. "Remember, come 5 minutes early," she said. I nodded and went over to where Amelia was sitting. When I found her, I was about to sit next to her as she put her hand up and shook her head.

"You can't sit here," she said, her voice cracking.

"Excuse me?" I asked, my heart dropping.

"Take a seat please," the bus driver said through clenched teeth.

I forced my legs to move toward an empty seat across the aisle from Amelia. As soon as I sat down, the bus started moving. Why would Amelia do that? I felt her eyes on me. Eventually she leaned over and whispered, "my mom and dad said we can't be friends or talk to each other anymore. I'm going to keep talking to you but when we're on the bus we can't sit with each other because my mom might see from her car as she's dropping me off at the bus stop." She took a deep breath.

"She thinks you're a bad influence now. If she knew I was talking to you, I'd be in so much trouble."

I turned to look at the window beside me in surprise. "What?!" I quietly exclaimed. I've known Amelia's parents for **two years.** They had always seemed so trusting and kind toward me. "Did your parents do anything else?" I whispered to Amelia's direction, knowing she was listening.

"You know my parents don't believe in spankings, so besides that, I got grounded for a month." She told me glancing around as if her parents were there. She lowered her voice to a quieter whisper. "How did you get punished?"

I tried to reply back quietly, even though I knew Amelia's mom couldn't possibly be on the bus with us or see us anymore. "My parents are actually giving me a week to prove I didn't make the banner. But I'm still grounded throughout this week and if I can't prove my innocence this week..." I gulped imagining the scenario.

Amelia didn't need me to finish that sentence as she nodded understandably. "Well, how are we going to prove we're innocent?" She asked fidgeting with her thumbs, like she does when she's nervous. She glanced around in paranoia again.

"Maggie's framed us," I said, spitting the words out. "She owns glittery pens and glitter markers. I saw her write a note in Mrs. Meanie's class and turn it in." Amelia's eyes widened. "No one else was called up to the principal but us, so that means she was definitely the one that turned us in. We both know we didn't do it so, that means she was lying in her note."

Amelia took off from there. "And the only reason to lie like that," she said excitedly, "was if she did it. Diamond, we just proved our innocence!" She said grinning.

I shook my head feeling bad about having to burst her bubble. "Think about it. Our main reason that we're innocent right now in the teacher's point of view is that she owns glitter markers and wrote the anonymous note. To actually get us out of trouble we're going to need better proof and an explanation as to why her craft material was found in *our* lockers."

Amelia looked at me, sadness almost coming over her, but then her face lit up once more. She leaned over and whispered in my ear. "Maggie's best friend – Kate! She heard us talking about knowing Maggie made the banner. She might have texted Maggie that she heard us saying that."

I nodded, "Giving her even more reason to frame us. We have to talk to Kate. Everywhere Maggie goes, she's there. Maybe, we can get her to confess that Maggie did it and catch it on camera!"

"But that's going to take time, effort and a bunch of luck. We're not supposed to even talk to each other. How are we supposed to pull this off?"

I smiled. "Like you said we're going to have to put time and effort. Maybe we can stay after school every day, with the excuse of attending Study Club, until we prove that we're innocent. I heard Kate's attends a lot, so she can copy homework answers from the smart kids." Amelia nodded slowly, with a thoughtful face. I continued, "I'll tell Kiara in first period. Let's start today. We only have seven days to prove our innocence until we face two weeks of lunch detention and no talent show."

"Yeah," Amelia said. "And that way, I'll be able to hang out with you, without my parents knowing. I'm allowed to go to Study Club even when I'm grounded."

"So am I," I said.

As we departed from the school bus, I walked to school with dread. News spreads fast and no doubt everybody had heard about us supposedly making the dumb, yellow banner. Sure enough, as I walked into the building, nearly 90% of the students and teachers were looking at me as if I was a criminal on the run. Everywhere I walked, I caught people snatching looks at me, quickly looking away.

I quickly dropped my things off at my locker and arrived at class in record timing, anxious to escape the accusing glares of the students in the hallway. As I walked in, Mrs. Meanie stared at me sadly as I pretended to dig in my backpack for a pencil. Everyone in my class was treating me the same as everyone else in the building. Kiara hadn't arrived yet, so I was shouldering the burden of the accusing stares alone. I desperately wished to escape from the building. Maybe I could run away and never come back. Maybe I could just get sucked up by the floor.

I sat sulking, in humiliating silence as everyone looked at me. I shifted my attention from self-pity to how I was going to tell Kiara about our after-school meeting at study club without breaking Mrs. Meanie's rule of silence before and during the morning announcements. Then once again, I thought about the possibility of failing in proving our innocence. I gulped and tried to divert my attention to something else as I fumbled for my calculator. My stomach rumbled and I winced remembering how I had skipped breakfast. Today was not going my way.

Fortunately, Kiara walked in then. I smiled at her, and she briefly smiled back as she sat at her desk. It was apparent that she was bummed out. I felt glad the attention of the accusing eyes was instantly divided between me and Kiara. As soon as the relief flooded within me, I felt like kicking myself for thinking that way. I then continued to chew on the problem of how to tell Kiara the information. Every other day, I have my lunch period with Kiara and the rest of the days, I share that period with Amelia. Unfortunately, I was having lunch with Amelia that day, and neither Kiara or Amelia have periods together, so Amelia couldn't even tell Kiara. This class was my only chance.

I continued to think about a solution and found a dangerous one – passing a note. I have never actually passed a note in my life, even though I've received many, so I was naturally nervous. I slowly took out a piece of paper and a pen, the entire time thinking, *the only thing that's next is tattoos and body piercings.*

To make matters worse, Maggie walked in. My anger bubbled up like a volcano. I fought the urge to walk over and slap her. She slowly walked over to her seat, smirking at me the entire time. Then she had the audacity to wink at me. No doubt was left in my mind that she knew that I knew that she did it. **And she had the audacity to wink at me!** At that moment, I felt Kiara beside me and her hand on my shoulder. She nodded. With that nod, I knew she knew that Maggie did it too. Somehow that calmed me down just enough for me to settle back to my seat.

Without anything else to do but pretend I didn't notice everybody staring at me, I took out a piece of paper and tried to start the note to Kiara. I picked up my pen and tried to bring it down to my paper. My hand wouldn't move. I tried again. Nothing. It was frozen.

Come on, I thought. My hand stubbornly stayed motionless. I was trying to calm myself by pointing out that the punishment for passing a note is only a call to your parents. *A phone call to your already seething mother,* my brain reminded me.

Imagine what would happen if she got a phone call about you passing a note. I shook the thoughts off and took a deep breath. I connected the pencil to the paper and nervously scribbled down information about our after-school Study Club meeting. Then I folded it in half, anxious for the note to leave my hands as soon as possible.

I scouted the room for a golden opportunity to pass the note without anyone finding out. Unfortunately, no opportunity came with me and Kiara being the center of attention and all. I let out a sigh and stuffed the note into my desk, so people didn't wonder why I was just awkwardly holding onto a piece of paper. While scouting the room, I imagined I looked like the most suspicious person ever. I dropped my head on my desk. This was way too stressful. *How does Kiara do this?*

I scouted the room once more. It seemed that more and more people were getting bored of Kiara and I, because less people were staring at us. A minute passed and Mrs. Meanie started fiddling with her computer. She then turned on the morning announcements. The two usual teachers popped on the screen, with their matching coffee cups and identical artificial smiles, talking about the lunch special for today (Sloppy Joes).

As the last few pairs of eyes turned away, I squeezed my eyes shut and reminded myself to take deep breaths. I snatched the note from the inside of my desk and quickly placed it on Kiara's desk. I hurriedly glanced across the room. No one had seen. I exhaled. A wave of confusion raced across Kiara's face as she picked up the note. She knew better than anyone how I felt about passing notes. She uncrumpled it, quickly read over it and gave me a thumbs up. It was official. Me, Amelia, and Kiara were going to prove our innocence.

Chapter 5

Chapter 7

HAPPILY EVER AFTER

O n the bus ride home, me and Amelia didn't talk to each other much. I looked out the window, she twiddled with her thumbs, and we were both aware of the glare Kate was throwing at us. When I finally arrived at home, I went straight to my room to find my bearings and flopped on my bed. Then, all of a sudden, I started crying. My crying turned into ugly crying, periodically interrupted by bursts of hiccups. I slammed my pillow on the ground, but it failed to calm me down.

After I couldn't cry anymore, I headed to my window, and opened it, letting the crisp, fall air cool my heated face. I started gulping in huge breaths of air as if I had never taken a full breath before. This made me feel slightly better. I headed back to my bed and flopped on it again. I knew I should start my homework but I was in no mood, so I left my backpack untouched.

I decided to take out a book and start reading. I think reading is one of the greatest treasures of the world. It takes you on an adventure that feels so real, like you're living it. You can read about sad, horrible things or joyful, happy things or romantic, lovey-dovey things. If the writer is good, you can laugh, cry, scream, and groan for the characters like they are your own family. So I opened the book, sniffling slightly.

I calmed down once I started reading. In my fiction world, I was going up with the characters to the dragon's lair. I laughed at Jack's sly remarks and cried at the death of Aria. But in the end, they defeated the dragon, found a potion that brought Aria back to life and lived happily ever after...

Happily ever after. Those words on the page jumped out at me and my eyesight was blurring from the tears welling up. I blinked rapidly, determined not to cry again. I slammed the book shut and threw it on my desk. There was one thing that most books had in common that simply isn't realistic. There's usually a happily ever after of some sort, and happily ever after doesn't always happen in real life. And it wasn't happening now. I glanced at the clock and sighed as I saw 2 hours had passed. I thought it was time to finally begin some English homework. I would do math later.

After struggling through my homework, groaning through Tennis practice, and absentmindedly eating dinner, I was sent to room as per my grounding. With nothing else to do but read, sleep, or do more homework, I decided to go straight to bed. I picked out my outfit for the next day and slept.

This time I fell into a sound sleep, but my mind wandered and I dreamt. I was walking on a tightrope and Maggie was shaking the rope viciously while laughing. Kate saw, took a step forward as if she was about to interfere but then she stopped, looked at me sadly, shook her head and walked away. Amelia, and Kiara were on the tightrope too and a horrible clacking of heels on tile echoed throughout the space. It sounded like it was getting closer. Bystanders that looked very much like the kids in my school looked on with terrified awe. A flute and saxophone danced around in the distance, balancing each other perfectly, playing a wonderful, sweet, sorrowful tune. But then the principal's high heel came and stomped on the floating instruments. The wonderful music ended. The flute and saxophone shattered.

I was struggling to balance; I was going to fall. I was falling! Everything was going by so fast. I felt dizzy so I squeezed my eyes shut. Then the fall abruptly ended. I opened my eyes timidly to discover I was bouncing. I had landed on a safety net. An enthusiastic and bright voice told me, "Don't give up yet." In the distance I saw the once shattered flute and saxophone get up and piece themselves together. They began to circle each other and then they began to dance again. The sad, sweet melody began to fill the air once more. I don't even know how this is possible, but it sounded even more in harmony than before. You couldn't tell what the flute played and what the saxophone played in this piece; it all blended. The voice as enthusiastic and bright as ever repeated what it said earlier. "Don't give up yet." Then, I woke up.

"Weird," I murmured to myself, yawning. I mean what do you say to a dream like that? I felt more at peace with myself than last night as I shrugged on my outfit. Even though everything seemed to be going wrong, something inside of me was saying I was going to be alright. I had no clue why I believed the intuition, but I did. Maybe it was the Friday vibes. I checked the clock and hoped I wasn't running late. I breathed a sigh of relief as I realized it was only 6:00 in the morning.

I took my time brushing my teeth and washing my face. I took extra time with my hair and tied it into a cute bun. I even slicked my baby hairs! Feeling pleased with myself, I headed downstairs, anxious to enjoy breakfast because I had missed it yesterday. I was excited to see we had biscuits from yesterday's dinner. I heated one up in the microwave and slathered an unhealthy amount of strawberry jelly on it. I grabbed my lunch quickly from the counter and decided to walk to the bus stop. I checked my watch – 6:55. Exactly 10 minutes before the bus would get there. I had plenty of time.

"Dad, can I walk to the bus stop today?" I asked walking into the kitchen.

"Sure," he replied while tying his tie.

"Have a nice day honey," my mom and dad told me in unison.

I smiled in gratitude and replied, "Have a good day at work!" I left, pulling on my favorite fall jacket and taking a big bite out of my biscuit. I munched happily, savoring the bite and the fresh fall breeze. I closed my eyes for a split second and I felt my foot trip over quite a large branch. "Whoa!" I exclaimed as I plummeted to the earth. Unable to properly stop the fall because I was carrying my biscuit, I fell roughly on my left knee. So much for the dumb dream. The spot on my knee that scratched the ground as I fell was starting to burn. I lifted my jeans to discover that it was scraped and already bleeding. My jeans were now starting to show a bit of blood and dirt among the denim blue. All of my school supplies were all over the floor too, since I didn't close my bag properly. I sighed, annoyed. What a great way to ruin a perfectly good morning.

"Whoa! Are you okay?" Someone asked. It was a boy's voice.

I looked up. I noticed two people that usually rode my bus, the boy who spoke and a girl. We had never talked before then, so I didn't know their names. "Yeah, yeah, I'm fine," I replied while scrambling to pick up my books.

I rolled my jean leg down to cover the scrape. I got up, zipped my backpack and put it on my shoulder. An awkward moment passed as we studied each other. The boy was super tall and skinny. His hair had a low fade and curls piled on the top. He wore bright red shorts and a green top that did not match. His outfit reminded me of one of a Christmas poster. The girl standing next to him was super tall with black hair cascading down her back. She wore black jeans, a black shirt, and a black jacket. I instantly thought of the middle school stereotypes with the gothic chicks huddled together during recess.

"At least your biscuit's okay," the girl noted. Confused, I looked down at my hand. A biscuit laid in my hand unharmed. Not a speck of strawberry jelly out of place. I had totally forgotten about it! I started laughing and then they started to laugh. I don't know why I couldn't stop laughing and apparently they couldn't either. Every time I stopped laughing, one look at them losing it would start me up again. And when they would stop, they'd glance at me and start up again.

We were already at the bus stop when we finally stopped laughing. Almost breathless from laughing, we took a few moments to control ourselves and calm our breathing. After our breathing had returned to normal, the girl bent down to re-tie her shoe and said, "What's your name?"

"Diamond," I replied. A wave of recognition passed over her face reminding me with a jolt how truly infamous I really was. My mood darkened.

"Aren't you the girl who got in trouble for supposedly making the yellow banner with your friends?" the boy asked fidgeting with his hands. Confused why he looked so guilty, my mind leapt into detective mode. Was he just very sympathetic or was that guilt on his face? And he used the word "supposedly" …What an interesting choice of word.

I studied his face closely as I said, "Yeah, I did get in trouble for it. But I didn't do it and my friends didn't either." A clearer wave of guilt washed over his face. I scraped my mind to see if I had ever seen him around Maggie before. I continued, "We were framed." This kid couldn't have looked guiltier if he tried to. Plus, his eyebrows raised on the word framed. Was that a clue? Did he frame us for Maggie? But Maggie told us she framed us herself. Maybe he knew something. What did he know? My mind was racing.

"I don't think you guys did it either," he said sheepishly. "By the way my sister's name is Ava." The bus pulled up then and we got on before I could question him further. It didn't really matter anyway. I could ask him questions later. Something told me this guy was the key to proving me, Amelia, and Kiara's innocence.

Anticipation Nation

Do you know that feeling that comes up when you're anxiously waiting for something? You're excited and you just wish that whatever you're waiting for shows up already. Every minute crawls around the clock like a snail. You check the clock in the back of the classroom occasionally. But every time you glance back there, only five minutes has passed. I'm talking about that horrible feeling of being trapped in slow motion and forced to live at a turtle's pace. Trapped in the hours of waiting, waiting, waiting…That was me all first period. I waited on needles and pins for Study Club to come around. Everything would go back to normal once we proved how Maggie framed us. I wouldn't be in trouble and get the accusing stares everywhere I went. Everyone would feel sorry that they accused Amelia, Kiara and I, *and* our reputations would be back!

This it all depended on Kate. I daydreamt about Kate agreeing to talk to the principal and turn Maggie in. When the bell rang, signaling the end of the period, I rushed out of Mrs. Meanie's class. Maggie sneered at me, and I sneered right back trying to keep my anger in check.

Then, third period (History) slowly creeped up. My thoughts tortured me with vivid images of sweet success and of utter failure. The time continued to limp along. Finally, History came to an end, and I hurried off to my locker to grab my lunch bag. My stomach rumbled and I quickly opened my locker and shoved my hand inside, but it closed around blank space. I look inside and noticed that my lunch bag wasn't there! I thought back to the morning and me rushing out the door. It was still at home.

I trudged to the cafeteria hungry and angry...hangry. The smells of the cafeteria taunted me, as if they were laughing at me. As I walked in, I became aware of all the pairs of eyes that were glancing at me and looking away. It was all Maggie's fault, and I was in no mood for any of it. I stormed in to find Amelia. I found her picking at her carrots at a table to the right of the cafeteria. As I walked over, she looked me over and broke into an expression of confusion. "What's up? It looks like you just ate poop," she said studying my face and then my hand. "Where's your lunch?"

"I left it at home. I was running late today," I said, sitting down next to her.

Amelia sighed sympathetically. "You can have my carrots. I hate carrots anyway."

"Thank you!" I exclaimed as I munched on the orange treats. To me, it felt like eating ice cream on a perfect summer day. I loved carrots. My anger slowly faded, but not entirely. After I had downed about three carrots, I looked Amelia in the eye and said with the greatest effect I could muster, "Let's go chew Maggie out."

"Huh?" Amelia asked, brushing her hair out of her face. "You mean try to get her to confess?"

"You know she'll never do that." I said. "No, I mean roast her, tell her we know she did it and we're going to find evidence…" The way Kiara was staring at me made me feel like an imbecile.

"Wouldn't that just tip her off that we're getting evidence to show she did it. If she didn't already thoroughly dust her tracks, she will if you go over there and tell her about it." She pointed her chin to the table Maggie was sitting at. She was still surrounded by almost every band, chorus, and instrumental student in the school. I looked away in disgust and faced Amelia again.

I felt stupid thinking that I could face Maggie that way. I decided to tell Amelia what had happened in Mrs. Meanie's classroom and why I was so angry in the moment. At that, Amelia got a little angry too, and that's saying something because she's not the type to allow her angry emotions surface. Her face broke into a frown, and she looked at me hard. "She knows we know she did it," Amelia repeated said, rubbing her temples. "And she *winked* at you."

I tacked a nod on the end of her sentence. She shook her head and sighed. "Fine, let's go over and talk to her. But only to ask if she really did it or not, and to find out if she'll confess. If she doesn't, we pretend we don't fully suspect her. But we will present the evidence to her and to the cafeteria, so everyone can consider the possibility that we didn't do it. You know, to get some of the public on our side." I nodded. It definitely wasn't the chewing out that I was wanting, but it would do just fine.

As we walked over to Maggie the crowd surrounding her parted like the red sea. Whispers and stares were abundantly in our direction. I tried to act like I didn't notice but it was quite difficult. Maggie had girls sitting on her right and left. I recognized one of them as Kate. The friends got up, left, and were lost in the sea of students. Amelia and I sat next to her stiffly and the crowd watched in shock. "What do you want?" Maggie whispered sternly. She probably knew why we were over there and didn't want her dirty little secret to come out.

I could tell Amelia noticed the same thing, because she said in a voice loud enough to reach the other side of the cafeteria, "Did you make the yellow banner and frame me, Kiara, and Diamond?"

A murmur spread throughout the crowd. Maggie did her best to look appalled, but she wasn't the best actor. "I did not frame you! You guys made the yellow banner, and I told the principal what I knew!"

"You and I both know that's not true," Amelia said. Another murmur rose in the crowd and Maggie started to look quite uncomfortable. She opened her mouth to retaliate but Amelia beat her to the punch.

"If you'd just admit that you framed us and tell the principal that *you* did it, you would still get the reduced punishment," Amelia said as if it was the best offer on earth. She sounded like one of the teachers on our morning announcements.

Maggie gasped as if we told her the world had run out of sparkly markers. "I saw you do it and I turned in a note like we were supposed to. Do you want me to break the rules, and lie for your benefit just so you won't be punished?" Another murmur went through the crowd, and this time the eyes were directed at me and Amelia. Then Maggie leaned in and said in a whisper that even we could barely hear, "I framed you, so what? But if you think I'm going to confess just like that, you're dumber than I thought. I heard you have a week to prove your innocence," she smirked and sarcastically said, "Good luck with that."

Amelia gasped and I stared at her taken aback that she had given a full-fledged confession. Then, I collected myself, realizing no one had heard and exclaimed, "Why, you little selfish brat! You really went through all of this, framed us, and made that yellow banner for a talent show? You know that you're lying! We're going to find evidence and then you'll be beside yourself, you snot brained, delusional, self-absorbed girl with an IQ equal to an empty bottle of glue," I said, riling up with all the insults.

Maggie held up her hand and did a "blah, blah, blah" motion with it. "What made you so angry?" Maggie exclaimed, acting shocked. The mini crowd murmured in agreement.

At this moment, I glanced at Amelia, and she looked as if she was about to blow, which was unusual for her. "You know what. I was going to give a nasty look but, I see you already have that covered," Amelia blurted. Maggie and the crowd looked as shocked as I was. She then quickly turned and walked away, and I quickly followed before Maggie retaliated.

Once we got back to the table, I pointed back at Maggie's table excitedly and put my hand up for a high five. "Did you see her face? I didn't know you had it in you to say something like that! Good for you!"

Amelia weakly gave me a high five and cast me a sad look. "Oh, don't remind me! I was just as bad as Maggie! I should go over and apologize." Amelia stood up soberly and moved to head over to Maggie's table.

I shook my head in amazement. "But she totally deserved it! You did nothing wrong but stand up for yourself!"

"I guess…" Amelia said, slowly sitting back down. "Did you hear what she said? She confessed! But I have a feeling there's almost no way she left any tracks that lead back to her."

I shook my head confidently. "That's not true. She left evidence with the people she told. You know she's a talkative person. She must've told someone and we're going to find out who. Then, we're going to get them to rat her out."

"Well, that shouldn't be too hard," Amelia said smiling playfully. I smiled and shrugged, "How hard can it be?"

Chapter 6

STUDY CLUB

L ater that day at school, I opened my locker hastily, shrugged my backpack on and walked to the library for Study Club. When I arrived, I was the first one there. The librarian gave me tons of strange looks, but I figured I must've looked weird. I mean, I had burst through the door, out of breath, with the small tidbit that it was known throughout the school that I supposedly made the yellow banner.

After a few minutes of impatient waiting, kids started to file in. It was mostly a mixture of kids who sincerely cared about their grades and people that were forced to be there by their parents. You can tell just by looking at them. The kid that cared about their grades would come holding necessary study supplies and a smile. The kid that was forced to be there would sneer, scowl and holding their a phone. Eventually, Amelia walked in, and I greeted her with a smile. "Hey," Amelia said sitting beside me in the small alcove of the library where Study Club was usually held. "Is Kate here?" she asked, taking out her lucky pencil and her notebook.

"No, not yet." I replied, fidgeting with the hair tie on my wrist. As I said this, Kiara walked in and sat across from us. An awkward moment passed as Kiara and Amelia studied each other. I realized that before this day, they had not met nor spoke, besides the locker interrogation we received from Mrs. Baxter. Awkward silence started to build up.

Finally, Amelia smiled and said "Hi, I'm Amelia."

"My name's Kiara."

They smiled at each other, and then more awkward silence persisted.

"So, um, what are your guys' favorite television shows?" I asked, already knowing both of their answers.

"Me and My Crazy Life," Kiara and Amelia said in unison.

"You like it too?" Amelia asked.

"Are you kidding? It's the best!" Kiara exclaimed.

We discussed the latest episode of "Me and My Crazy Life", while we kept our eye on the door for Kate. About five minutes into the conversation, Kate burst in the library looking very happy to be there. I studied her for a minute and wasn't sure if she was there to study or not. There were no study materials in her hand. Instead, she bore the latest edition of Teen Magazine. She donned the widest smile and bright blue headphones around her neck. Sticking out of her back pocket was a blue phone. She wore black, shiny, boots, with a huge heel. Her lips were slathered with a pink lip gloss that looked more like lipstick. She had shorts that stopped right where her thigh began…my mother would kill me if my shorts were that short. She wore a crop top that had bright black words spelling, "You wish you were me". Now that I think about it, she really looked and dressed like Maggie.

She plopped down at a table by herself, opened her magazine and started reading. We glanced at each other, all asking the same question without words, "How were we going to get Kate to confess?"

I decided to initiate discussing the plan. In a lowered voice, I huddled with the others and said, "So, to get down to business, how in the world are we supposed to get Kate to confess? I hope she knows that Maggie did it."

"Wait. Hold on a minute. Are we absolutely certain that Maggie did it?" Kiara asked. "I know we have our reasons, and we know that she would have told Kate everything. But we shouldn't count everyone else out until we get really solid proof that Maggie did it."

I realized that Kiara didn't know what happened at the cafeteria yet. I was about to fill her in when Amelia jumped in. "Actually, we do have solid proof. Maggie confessed to me and Diamond. She said that it was her who made the yellow banner and framed us all." Kiara didn't even look surprised. I mean all of us have known Maggie for years and we knew that she can go to great lengths to get what she wants.

"But that wasn't a confession. It was bragging," Kiara said.

"Exactly. She's not going to confess. Our only lead is the people she might've told. Since Kate is her best friend and Maggie likes to run her mouth, I'm almost certain she told her. Now, how are we supposed to coax Kate into confessing for Maggie?" I said rubbing my hand over my chin like they do with beards in television shows.

"I think we should tell her we know Maggie did it and secretly record her reaction to see if she confesses. I can record her. I'll just place my phone under the table," Kiara said.

"Wow. That's actually super smart!" I exclaimed, not realizing that it was a huge breech of Kate's privacy.

Kiara flashed me a smile, nodded smugly and said, "I know."

"It is a really great idea," Amelia concurred.

I grinned. "Well, if anybody has anything to say about this plan, speak now or forever hold your peace." Nobody spoke. I clapped my hands together and smiled. "Time to prove our innocence."

We walked over to Kate, trying to look as natural as possible. Amelia kept breaking into a grin and then started looking very solemn. Kiara kept fidgeting with her hands, grinning as if she won the lottery. I don't know what I looked like, but I felt exhilarated, scared, and extremely nervous. As we got closer to Kate's table, she peeped over her magazine and stared at us with wide eyes.

After what felt like forever, we arrived at Kate's table. I nervously cleared my throat and said in my most confident voice. "Hey, Kate. Can we sit here?"

Kate stared at us as if studying our motives and replied very nervously, "Yes." Amelia, Kiara and I sat down at her table. I saw Kiara slip her phone under the table out of the corner of my eye. Kate looked at us and said, "So, why are you guys in Study Club?"

Kiara answered without missing a beat, "English. You know that English paper we have to write about one thing that changed our lives for the better? I'm having so much trouble with that!" She laughed, Kate smiled and then nervously laughed along. Me and Amelia laughed too, even though we knew it was a partial lie. She was having trouble with the paper but that wasn't why we were *really* here.

Kate smiled and said, "I'm studying for Spanish. I don't really need to because I don't have that much trouble with it. But it's such a beautiful language! I come here almost every day so I can study Spanish or do some other homework. It calms me and relaxes me. Plus, it beats just sitting at home!" She spoke so passionately about Spanish that I was moved. But, how does someone study with a fashion magazine? Is she really lying to our faces? I decided to ask her.

"That's super cool but how are you studying for Spanish with a magazine?" I asked.

Kate giggled and said, "It helps me learn Spanish because it's written in Spanish. I would rather read something else, but this is all I have for now." She slid the magazine over to me. I opened it skeptically, but sure enough the words were entirely in Spanish.

"Wow! You understand all of this!" I exclaimed. Kate nodded shyly.

"That's really cool!" Amelia agreed.

Kiara then made a "hurry it up" signal with her hands. I took a deep breath and looked Kate in the eye.

"Kate, you know how me, Amelia, and Kiara have one week to prove that we didn't make the yellow banner before we get punished?" Kate slowly nodded her head. "Well, we really are innocent, and we know Maggie framed us." Kate's eyes widened like a deer in headlights. "You know it too. Don't you?" Kate said nothing. I took a deep breath and continued. "Can you admit to the principal that Maggie framed us and made the yellow banner?"

Kate stared at us like the guiltiest person in the world and said, "I-I-I don't know what you're talking about." She was obviously lying. "Maggie might not be the nicest person in the world but she's like my sister and I wouldn't say anything to hurt her." Kate took a deep breath, "I'm sorry that I can't help you." While she said this, her elbow knocked her magazine to the ground underneath the table.

"I'll get it!" Amelia said hurriedly swooping under the table, but it was too late. Kate picked up her magazine and spotted Kiara's phone recording.

Her mouth rounded into a surprised, little "O". "Oh my goodness!" She exclaimed. She glared at us, and her face crumpled into an expression of anger. "You were recording! You only wanted to talk to me to record me without my permission, so you can prove that you're innocent! You know that's illegal right? Maggie was right about you guys being horrible people. I shouldn't have been talking to you!"

"But, Kate, she framed us and you can help! Keeping a lie is as bad as telling one."

"Did you just call me a liar? You guys were the ones breaking the law, not me!" I could feel the now familiar number of people staring at us increase. "You know what, just leave!" Kate her voice cracking.

I looked around. Too many people were watching. If we didn't leave, we wouldn't only be in trouble for making the yellow banner; we would also be in trouble for breaking the law. I slowly got up while Amelia and Kiara followed. We left the table to head back to our own. I glanced back and Kate looked truly hurt. I felt like kicking myself. Kate didn't deserve this. Once we got back to the table, I slumped down and covered my head with my hands. Kiara stared at us guiltily, let out a deep breath and said "Sorry guys. I shouldn't have proposed that we record Kate."

I shook my head. "It's not your fault. We shouldn't have gone along with the idea."

"Yeah," Amelia agreed, "Friends are supposed to stop each other from doing stupid stuff."

Kiara kicked the carpet. "Now Maggie and Kate both hate us."

"I feel really bad too!" I exclaimed.

"Plus, we're all dead now. There is no one else Maggie would trust to tell something that momentous to other than Kate," Amelia added.

"We can't just give up`. She couldn't have covered *all* of her tracks," I said half-heartedly.

"Yeah, maybe," Kiara agreed, sighing.

"Well, Study Club is about to be over," Amelia pointed out, looking at the clock. "Same time and place tomorrow?" Amelia asked.

"Sure," Me and Kiara mumbled, as the bell rang announcing that it was time to go home.

Chapter 8

MRS. MEANIE

I walked in the bus and sat across from Amelia with a smile on my face. "Someone's happy," Amelia noted. I nodded and took a bite out of my biscuit.

"Yup," I said smiling. I broke her off a piece of my biscuit and handed it to her.

"Thanks."

"No problem," I replied. "Now, do you know who Max is?"

"No," Amelia replied, taking a bite out of the piece of biscuit I gave her.

"Well, he's a boy at my bus stop and I think he knows Maggie framed us." Amelia raised her eyebrows. "Hear me out. I talked to him, and he doesn't believe we made the yellow banner. When I told him we were framed, he looked like the guiltiest person on earth."

Amelia frowned. "Well, that's nowhere near solid proof but it's the only lead we have, so I guess we should look into it. Does he go to Study Club?"

"I don't know," I replied. "I don't have a class with him and neither do you so we can't really question him if he doesn't go to Study Club. But maybe Kiara has a class with him."

"Maybe," Amelia replied. "If she does have a class with him tell her absolutely no recording allowed if she questions him."

"Yeah," I said grimacing while remembering yesterday. "That was a huge mistake." I glanced behind me and saw Kate staring out the window looking every bit as sad and as hurt as yesterday.

"Well, let's not talk about any of that anymore," Amelia said sighing. "I'm so sick with anything involving the yellow banner and the talent show."

I nodded in agreement. "Anything new with you?" I asked, changing the subject.

"Actually yes," she said beaming. "Yesterday I had a really great basketball practice."

"What happened?"

"Well," she said beaming, "I was playing point guard against the best defender on our team, and she sprained her ankle...pretty bad," she added softly. I could tell she was super proud of herself, but she didn't want to seem cocky.

"Whoa," I said, gaping at her. "That's awesome." I felt the tiniest bit of jealousy surge up in me. "I haven't been doing too good in tennis lately," I said sighing.

"That's okay," she responded good naturedly. "Everybody hits a rough spot." After that, we talked about random stuff, like the show "Me and My Crazy Life," and the shape of the clouds.

The bus pulled up to the school in what felt like two seconds and we parted ways to go to our classes. Walking to my first period class, I felt some stares from students but not as much as yesterday.

I entered Mrs. Meanie's classroom and sat at my usual spot. I looked at the board that was updated daily with what homework was due. Written in bold letters it said, "Math project due today". I was done for – I didn't have my project completed. Everyone knows Mrs. Meanie hates late work. She despises it only a little less than she hates students passing notes. At least she doesn't call your parents. I started creating a scenario in my mind about how the next few minutes would look like for me.

"Okay," Mrs. Meanie declared, clearing her throat. "I will now begin collecting the math project that is due today." She'll walk around the neat row of desks collecting the math projects. Then when she comes to my desk, she'll see that there is no paper on my desk to be collected. "Take out

your math project please," she'll say sternly, looking over the rim of her glasses knowing there was nothing to take out.

"I left it at home," I'll stammer.

She'll purse her lips together and look at me in disbelief. "Hmmm," she'll say while the entire class would hold in snickers behind their hands. "I expect it by tomorrow, Diamond. I will be taking off points."

"Diamond!" Mrs. Meanie snapped loudly. I snapped out of my daydream. "Yes, Mrs. Me-Johnson," I replied.

Mrs. Meanie glared at me, but I don't think she heard me almost call her "Mrs. Meanie". "Answer my question please," her eyes twinkled knowing she was delivering a punishment worse than detention. She knew perfectly well I had no idea what she said. She just wanted to embarrass me in front of the class. I refused to give her the satisfaction.

"I'm sorry. I didn't hear you," I responded boldly, talking slowly, loudly, and clearly so I wouldn't do something stupid like stutter. I looked around the classroom. The class was watching like this was the best movie they'd ever seen. But I couldn't blame them. Someone getting in trouble is a lot more interesting than fractions. Both Kiara and Maggie had arrived while I was daydreaming. Kiara cast me a sympathetic glance.

"I don't appreciate my students not paying attention in class." Mrs. Meanie stated. I nodded my head meekly. "The question I asked you is, 'Where is your math project?'"

71

I gulped. "I left it at h-home," I said softly. So much for not giving her the satisfaction of stuttering.

Mrs. Meanie cast me a look that made my knees wobble. I had just committed two humongous crimes in her book. I had not paid attention in her class, and I didn't have my project to turn in on time. "Hmmm," Mrs. Meanie said in utter disbelief. She obviously thought I was lying about leaving my project at home. My daydream was coming true. "I expect it by tomorrow. I will be taking off a letter-grade." She then walked away to the next desk. I looked around the room again. Every single pair of eyes were on me. I groaned, forced to wallow in shame and sit in silence.

I felt a tingle in the back of my brain. *"You're forgetting something. You know what could end the stares, right?"* I whispered back, *"What?"*

"I see I'm going to have to spell this out for you. You prove yourself innocent and the stares will end forever…unless you get in trouble again.

"Okay, and?" I reply back.

"Remember, you think Max knows something about the framing, and you want to ask Kiara if he's in any of her classes.

"Ohhh…right. But we're not allowed to talk in Mrs. Meanie's class," I say.

"That's what notes are for, right?"

"Stop, I'll get in trouble."

"No, you won't, you'll be fine. Look to your left, they're passing notes right now! Nobody gets caught," my brain argued.

Part of me thought this was stupid. But the other part of me realized I hadn't asked Kiara if she had a class with Max yet. I did have multiple classes with her so I could tell her later that day, but I was too excited to wait any longer. I would just have to pass a note again. I knew if I was caught, I'd be absolutely dead, but I was confident I wouldn't get caught. I scribbled out a brief note describing my hunch that Max knew vital information that would prove we were innocent. In the note, I asked her if she had a class with him. I looked around the classroom to see if anyone was looking at me. No one was. I passed it quickly to Kiara's desk. I looked around. I breathed a sigh of relief as I scanned the classroom and then I saw Maggie looking right at me. Our eyes locked. Her mouth twisted into a sneer. She had seen me passing the note…I was so dead.

Maggie raised her hand high. Mrs. Meanie smiled and nodded her head at Maggie, signaling her to speak. I braced myself for the words. Loud, clear and with a sneer on her lips, Maggie promptly said, "Diamond passed a note!" The whole class whipped their heads to me. I felt my cheeks burn in shame. I had committed my third major crime that morning and I knew I would pay severely for it. After all, three strikes and you're out. Out of the corner of my eye I saw Kiara scribbling on the back of the note frantically.

"Is this true Diamond?" Mrs. Meanie said, walking toward me like a cat to its prey. I nodded my head shakily. "Who did you pass this note to?"

"Kiara," I mumbled.

"Kiara, please hand me the note." Kiara walked to the teacher and handed her the note and quickly shuffled back to her seat The teacher read the note quickly and her face broke into one of sympathy? "Diamond, if you have questions about the class or subject, please ask me. I am here to help. Since your note you passed was a question about the class, I will only give you a warning." I was so confused I felt like the world was spinning. I looked over at Kiara and she winked. Kiara had changed the note!

"To answer your question, you always solve the groupings first in Order of Operations. Remember GEMDAS. First you solve groupings, then exponents, then multiplication and division, and *then* addition and subtraction." Mrs. Meanie said with a smile. "I stay after school on Tuesdays if you need help," she said addressing the class. Then she turned back to her desk and promptly threw the note in her trash can. Maggie looked like her birthday party just got cancelled. I stuck my tongue out at her.

The rest of math class was thankfully uneventful. I did notice that we went over order of operations quite a bit that day. Did the teacher think I was stupid? Or worse… Did the class think I was stupid? I decided to raise my hand more than I usually do and answer questions on Order of Operations.

First period ended uneventfully and so did second period. Then it was finally time for lunch. Walking to lunch, I remembered how I still needed to ask Kiara if she had Max in any of her classes, since she couldn't respond to my note. I cringed remembering how close I was to getting caught. Kiara had saved my skin. I totally needed to thank her for that. I walked to lunch with a skip in my step.

When I arrived at lunch, I saw Kiara sitting at our usual table. I walked over to her with a smile on my face. "Hey Kiara. Thanks for changing the note," I said sitting down at the table.

"No problem," Kiara replied, sipping on her water bottle. "Oh, and about your note. I don't know who Max is. Can you describe him so I can make sure if he's in any of my classes?"

I nodded my head thinking back on how he looked. "Well, he's tall and skinny. He has a low fade. He wore super bright colors…" I said.

"Hmm," Kiara said scratching her head and looking around. "Hey, that looks like the kid you just described," Kiara noted pointing at the water fountain. I whipped my head around to look at the water fountain. Standing there filling up his water fountain was none other than Max. My mouth rounded into a perfect round "O".

"Kiara, you have got to be the luckiest person in the world," I said shocked. "That's the kid I was describing. That's Max!"

It was Kiara's turn to be surprised. "What a coincidence."

"Not a coincidence. It's fate! I know he knows something!" I said getting excited. "We have to talk to him!" I stood up excitedly.

Kiara put down her water bottle. "Wait, what. What are we supposed to say? Shouldn't we plan something out or something?"

"Look where planning's gotten us so far," I said thinking about Kate.

Kiara nodded and stood up. "You're right," Kiara said. "But we need to have a small version of a plan," she said. "How about good cop/bad cop? I'm bad cop."

"Sure whatever. But hurry up, he's about to leave the water fountain!" I exclaimed. We sped-walked toward the water fountain just as he was putting on the cap. We got there right before he left. "Hi Max," I said, acting as if I had just seen him.

"Hey," he said, starting to walk away.

"Can I ask you a question?" Kiara asked coldly.

"Sure," Max said, starting to look nervous and extremely guilty. He was fidgeting with his hands. He had to know something. Kiara passed me a glance that said she noticed this as well.

"Do you know who framed us?" Kiara asked point-blank, crossing her hands over her chest. She didn't even try to beat around the bush. Max fidgeted with his hands and his breath was coming out fast. "Don't lie to us," Kiara added.

Max slumped and seemed less tall. "Well, not really," he muttered.

"What do you mean by that?" I asked.

Max looked around scouting the lunchroom. He whipped out his phone and unlocked it quicker than even Kiara. He pulled out a video on his phone. He slowly hit play. "Welcome back to my YouTube channel," Max said in the video, with a background that looked like our school lockers. "So, my opinion on…" a loud clunk sounded off close by. "Ugh, now I'm going to have to reshoot," Max muttered. "I'm asking whoever made that noise to keep it down." He grabbed the phone and walked toward the noise. He continued recording.

He turned the corner toward the sound of the noise. I gasped with Max in the video as I saw someone dressed in all black shoving large pieces of yellow banner paper into a locker. The person didn't seem to hear the gasp from Max. The person went on shoving the neatly folded pieces of yellow banner just right so it could fit into slots of the locker. Obviously, a lot of thought had went into this. The person shoved a few glittery markers in the slots as well. I looked closer and saw that it was none other than my locker! The person stealthily moved away to Kiara and Amelia's locker and did the same. Max followed the person recording it all. After all, three of the lockers were done with the person dashed off. As the person turned and ran away you could see the face for a split second. "Pause the video," I exclaimed. We were finally going to have solid evidence that Maggie framed us once and for all!

Chapter 9

EVIDENCE

Max paused the video. My face settled on a mask. A very large black mask that covered the entire face. I knew who was behind the mask. But there was no way for anyone else who saw the video to know. Maggie really was an expert at covering her tracks. I sighed. But I forced away my anger. It didn't matter anyway. We had concrete evidence that someone had framed us. I wouldn't get in trouble, I could enter the talent show with Kiara, and I wouldn't be known as the bad kid anymore. No more suspicious stares or accusing glances. I would be able to freely be friends with Amelia again. Everything would just be normal. And all of this happened because I had decided to take the bus today.

Kiara smiled and said, "Max this is great!" Then her face darkened. "But why wouldn't you tell the principal? If you had this all this time, why wouldn't you say anything?" Kiara demanded. I hadn't even thought of that! I glared at him as well.

"Well, you know phones aren't allowed. I would get in trouble." He said pathetically, throwing up his hands. "Plus, I was supposed to be in gym class, not recording my YouTube video." I rolled my eyes. "Anyways, I just wanted to show you guys the video so you knew you were framed. I'm still not showing it to the principal or anything."

"What?" I practically screamed. I sensed a few heads turning our way. "We already knew that we were framed, so thanks for nothing! Anyway, if you show the video to the principal, they'll be a lot more concerned with the person framing us than punishing you," I exclaimed. "Now that you recorded that person framing us, the only choice is to show the principal. You're involved in our problem, like it or not!"

Max shook his head, "Sorry guys." He turned and walked away. Just like that, the chance of proving ourselves as innocent was lit and then abruptly stomped out. Like the heel in my dream, I thought gasping. Maybe my dream was a sign.

"Max," Kiara called after him, "if you don't do the right thing, it will lay on you for the rest of your life," she said angrily. He didn't even look back. We weren't going to be able to prove our innocence. I wasn't going to be able to talk to Amelia without going behind her parents back. I wouldn't be able to compete in the talent show. I would get lunch detention and the accusing stares would never stop. It was suddenly all too much for me. I felt my eyes beginning to water. Kiara looked at me worried. "Are you okay?" she asked.

"Yeah, yeah, I'm fine" I muttered. "I just need to go to the bathroom." I desperately needed to get out of there. Kiara nodded as if she understood. I stormed out of the cafeteria and into the bathroom. I locked myself into a stall and struggled to get deep breaths in. When did breathing get so hard? A single tear slithered down my cheek. I wiped it away quickly. "Crying doesn't fix anything," I muttered to myself. I tried to smile. My cheeks felt like they weighed a thousand pounds each. But I had read somewhere that smiling tricked the body into thinking that it was happy. It certainly wasn't working for me.

I took another deep breath. "Maybe, I'll find someone else who knows something," I told myself. Nothing sounded more like a lie. "Friday vibes," I said, trying to be happy. "Friday vibes, Friday vibes, Friday… oh no!" I unlocked the stall door hurriedly. "Today is our last school day to prove our innocence and we're basically back at square one! Lunch detention starts on Monday. How could I forget? We're so dead!" I murmured. A girl walked into the bathroom which ended my pity party. I had probably stayed in there too long as it was anyway. I checked the mirror hoping my eyes weren't red. They were slightly pink but at a glance, you couldn't tell anything was wrong. I sighed and briskly walked out of the bathroom to resume the nightmare that was my life.

I walked back to the cafeteria and took a seat at my lunch table with Kiara. "We're dead," I murmured. She nodded her head in agreement.

"So very dead." Then her eyes lit up. "Unless… I nodded for her to go on. "We could steal his phone."

"What? Kiara I'm not a thief," I said.

Kiara nodded her head. "Yeah, that's wrong. I guess I was getting kind of desperate. Anyway, lunch detentions aren't that bad."

"And the talent shows not that great anyway," I added.

"They have elimination rounds tomorrow before school, right?" she asked.

I nodded glumly.

"And aren't they announcing the grand prize Monday?" Kiara added.

"Yeah, but I bet it'll be really lame. Like maybe a slice of cold pizza," I said laughing.

"Yeah, or a class with a tutor," Kiara said laughing.

"Oh, or maybe a piece of gum," I said.

"Or a, umm oh I know! A bar of used deodorant," she said laughing. I died at that one. By the time lunch ended I felt way better. The rest of the day was uneventful. At the end of the day, walking out of the building to my bus, I looked back at my school knowing that on Monday when I walked in, my punishment would officially start. I would forever be known as the kid who made the yellow banner. I sighed, readjusted my backpack on my shoulder and headed toward my bus. I entered, saw Max, glared at him, and sat down across from Amelia.

"Did Kiara have a class with Max?" Amelia asked.

"Yup," I said, sighing knowing I would have to relive the event. "Turns out I have a class with him too – lunch."

"Well, what happened?" Amelia asked on the edge of her seat. The engine of the bus revved up and started on the course home.

"Well, my hunch was correct. When we questioned Max, he showed us a video of Maggie putting the stuff in our lockers. You couldn't tell it was Maggie though, because she had on a black mask that completely covered her face. Nevertheless, it's very concrete evidence that could get us out of this mess in a snap." Amelia's face lit up. I took a deep breath. It was time to cover the hard part. "But he's not going to show the principal. He's afraid he'll get in trouble for using his phone in school and lying about being on a bathroom break to film his YouTube channel."

Amelia's hand flew to her mouth. "Well, that's it then. All our leads are dead ends, and we only have until Monday." She sighed loudly. "And it's Friday."

"Yeah, we're dead," I replied.

Amelia sighed, "I thought this would happen. I thought we wouldn't be able to prove that we didn't make the yellow banner. But now that it's actually happening… It's just so…," she paused and took a deep breath, "sad." I nodded in agreement. We then rode in silence until it was our time to get off the bus. I was going to wave goodbye to her, but I stopped myself as I saw that her mom had come to pick her up. It was a painful reminder how I wasn't allowed to be her friend. I trudged home, opened the door and went straight to my room.

The weekend trudged along slower than a snail ever could. I sat in my room all day because I was grounded. I read and did homework to occupy the time, but it eventually got boring. With nothing to take my mind off of Monday, it was the only thing I could think about. Lunch detention, public humiliation, and a huge punishment from my parents after school was in my inevitable future and I was not looking forward to it. Tossing in my bed on Sunday night I desperately wished for pink eye, a dreadful stomach bug, or a horrible migraine to stop me from going to school. After about an hour of worrying about Monday, I finally fell asleep.

My alarm sounded, bringing me back to reality with a jolt. I groggily sat up and walked over to the mirror. My eye couldn't have been even close to a shade of pink and I felt perfectly fine. I sighed, as I slipped into a sweater and a pair of jeans. Then I walked to the bathroom, brushed my teeth, and washed my face. I slipped my backpack on my shoulder and looked into the mirror sadly. Then I checked my watch. It was 6:50. I had 15 minutes until I had to be at the bus stop. My brain also calculated that I had 10 minutes to be at the school for the talent show elimination rounds. I brushed the thought away knowing perfectly well that I wasn't going.

I walked downstairs and popped a piece of toast in the toaster. "Diamond, after school today, you're going to have to be punished for making the yellow banner," my mom said sadly.

"Yes, mom," I responded glumly. The toast then popped out of the toaster with gusto. I slathered jelly on it and glanced at my watch. 10 minutes until I had to be at the bus stop. I could walk there. There was something I wanted to say to Max. "Can I walk to the bus stop?" I asked my dad.

"Of course," my dad responded. Then my mom and dad both called out to me, "Have a good day at school."

"I will," I responded as I walked out the door. I had lied to myself quite a bit over the last school week about things clearing up for me, but that one definitely took the cake. A breeze blew, reminding everybody that winter would conquer fall soon. I hugged my sweater closer to my body. Fall seemed to respond by moving the sun from behind the clouds, giving us hope that winter hadn't won yet. I quickened my walking pace so I could talk to Max before the bus pulled up. Halfway to the bus stop I saw Max. He was ahead of me, and it didn't look like he had seen me yet. His sister wasn't with him today. Maybe *she* got pink eye. Some people get all the luck. I quickened my pace even more. I was only about a step behind him when he turned around and noticed me. His eyes went wide. "Hello Max," I said coldly.

"Hello," he said nervously. He was obviously wondering why I was talking to him. I decided to cut to the chase.

"You might not think hiding the video from the principal has no consequences on your part. But it does. You will forever have to live with the fact that you helped ruin a friendship," I said thinking of Amelia. "You let someone who deserves to be punished walk away untouched," I continued thinking of Maggie. "You got three innocent people lunch detention and a ruined reputation. Not to even mention no participation in the talent show!" I was beyond angry at this guy, and he needed to understand what he was doing. "The principal needs to know the truth, the teachers need to know the truth and the students need to know the truth!" I sounded like a cheesy T.V. show but I couldn't care less.

"It's too late to show the video now," he mumbled looking at the floor.

"No, it's not!" I replied, raising my voice. "If you'd just show the principal the video you will be helping me, Amelia and Kiara more than you know," I said every word as if it was a dagger aimed at his chest. I closed my eyes to calm down. All I saw was red. "But it's your decision," I said through my teeth as I walked away toward the bus stop.

Chapter 10

MAX'S P.O.V.

The girl's words left me standing there speechless as she walked away. I felt like a horrible person, but I just couldn't do it. I would get in so much trouble if I showed the principal the video. Everyone would ask me why I hadn't shown them the video sooner. Not to mention my parents disappointment. I would never be able to face them again. They would take away my YouTube channel!

But then I thought of Diamonds face as she spoke to me. I thought of her words. I shook my head and walked towards the bus stop trying to forget them, but they were torturous. Especially the sentence, *"if you'd just show the principal the video you will be helping me, Amelia and Kiara more than you know."* I didn't know what to do. If I kept my mouth shut it would be like I never filmed the video in the first place. But I would know I had.

I clutched my phone in my hand, caressing it with my fingers. My thoughts swirled around in my head battling each other. Finally, the bus arrived, and I got on. I sat in a seat by myself in the back so I could think in peace. No matter how hard I thought I didn't know what to do. The bus arrived at school way too soon, and I still didn't know what to do. In first, period I pretended to pay attention to English class as I continued to contemplate what I was going to do. Diamond's words raged in my head. First period was over before I knew it, and I was on my way to second. My thoughts were banging against my skull, each one fighting for my attention throughout this period as well. I knew it was my last chance to confess because lunch was after this period. The sentence replayed in my mind like a broken radio over and over and over, *"If you'd just show the principal the video you will be helping me, Amelia and Kiara more than you know."*

Almost mechanically I raised my hand. "Yes, Max," Mrs. Jones said smiling at me. I didn't deserve to be smiled at.

"May I go to the principal's office," I said, trying hard to keep my voice steady. I touched my phone laying innocently in my pocket. I felt like I was touching an atomic bomb.

"Why?" Mrs. Jones prodded.

"I have vital information regarding the case of the yellow banner," I said as if I was a lawyer stating my case. A wave of murmuring spread over the classroom.

Mrs. Jones nodded and said, "Then you may."

I left the classroom and walked down the hall towards the principal's office. When did the hall get so long? When did it get so hard to walk? When did it get so hard to breathe? At the principal's door, I paused. I could turn back now. I didn't have to do this. I remembered Diamond's words. I pushed open the door.

"Why have you come to see me?" The principal asked. I took a deep breath and slowly unlocked my phone. She looked extremely confused. I located the video and then I pressed play.

Chapter 11

THE OFFICE

In P.E while everyone was stretching, the screechy intercom said, "Can Amelia Anderson and Diamond Smith report to the principal's office?" The exact same words that made my life spin out of control all those days ago. Although this time the voice sounded much nicer. A murmur spread throughout the classroom like fire. I gulped and glanced at Amelia. She looked at me and shrugged. As soon as we got out of the gym doors I said, "Do you know why we got called to the office?"

Amelia shook her head in worry. "Maybe they changed their mind and they decided to expel us instead of giving us lunch detention!" I gulped. That *was* a possibility. We hadn't had the best of luck recently.

We walked to the principal's office nervously. I can't say what Amelia was thinking because I don't know, but I was thinking about what could possibly go wrong in the principal's office. Judging from her face, I think she was too. We walked in the principal's office to find an uncomfortable looking Maggie, a beaming Kiara and a confused Max. I say Max was confused because he transferred between looks of happiness, fear, and nervousness.

I sat down next to Kiara and Amelia sat down next to me. I noticed Max's phone on the principal's table. Had he… "Ladies you were called here because Max showed us very interesting footage," the principal said breaking my train of thought. "Max, can you pull up the video?" The principal said. Max nodded his head and quickly pulled out his phone. The video showed someone in a black mask putting the items in our three lockers. I looked at Maggie and her eyes were growing wider and wider every second that the video was playing. When it ended there was a brief silence in the room.

Then the principal cleared her throat. She said, "Amelia, Diamond and Kiara, this proves that you didn't make the yellow banner. I am so sorry for anything you may have endured through this week because of this issue. You are not to report to lunch detention, and you will be able to participate in the talent show." My face split into a huge, elated smile. Then the principal sighed, "But as you know the talent show elimination rounds were held this morning, so I am not sure if there are spots left at all for the talent show." After all of this we might not even get a chance to participate! I felt my heart sinking in my chest. "Please see Mrs. Garcia and ask her if there are any spots left, should you want to participate in the talent show. Again, I am so sorry for everything. I will notify your parents that you did not make the yellow banner." She smiled at us with sympathy. "You may now return to class. Max and Maggie please stay."

As we left, I saw the principal turn toward Maggie with a frown. Then I heard "Maggie, you said that you saw Amelia, Kiara and Diamond make the yellow banner. We now know this cannot be true which means that you lied. Why did you lie?" She said harshly. I imagined with a smile how uncomfortable Maggie must be feeling. How was she going to talk her way out of this one I wondered? I heard stammering from Maggie as I closed the door on my way out. Let her suffer!

I looked at Kiara and we shared a grin. Then I looked at Amelia. Her smile beamed and sparkled like a million stars. We walked in silence bathing in the glory of not being guilty. Then I said, "I can't believe Max showed the video to the principal."

Kiara shook her head in awe, "On Friday it looked like he couldn't care less!"

"Maybe, my words got through to him," I murmured.

"What?" Amelia asked, beaming her wonderful smile my way.

"I kind of talked to Max about the video before we got on the bus today," I said beaming because it had worked.

"Ooooooh," Kiara and Amelia said together.

"What's that supposed to mean?" I said putting my hands on my hip.

"Well, it means that if you talked to him, I would've been surprised if he didn't show the principal the video," Kiara said.

Amelia nodded, "Yeah, when you get angry…" she shook her head and chuckled. Was I really a hot head? I pushed it out of my mind as I remembered the second half of the principal's speech.

"Do you think there's going to be spots left for the talent show?" I asked the group. Amelia and Kiara shrugged.

"Who knows," Amelia sighed, shrugging. "Let's ask Mrs. Garcia after school today. Right before we go home." Me and Kiara nodded in agreement.

"See ya," Kiara said as she turned a corner toward her class. Me and Amelia waved goodbye and walked into P.E. The rest of the day went surprisingly well for school. It felt wonderful telling people what happened in the principal's office. Throughout the day, I wondered how I would tell my parents what happened in the principal's office. I could already picture the relief on their faces. I was really looking forward to that moment. Anyway, the end of the day came up fast, so before I knew it, I was walking to Mrs. Garcia's office with Kiara and Amelia by my side.

"I'm nervous," Amelia said, biting her lip as we headed toward Mrs. Garcia's office.

"There'll be spots for both of us though. I just know it," Kiara replied as we turned a corner.

"Even if there aren't any spots left, I'm just glad we cleared our names," I said mentally preparing myself for disappointment.

"Yeah, me too," Amelia and Kiara agreed. We walked in silence for a couple more steps until we saw Mrs. Garcia's office. In unison we let out a shaky breath and walked inside.

"Hello girls," Mrs. Garcia said while shuffling papers on her desk. She looked very busy. She spoke in a rushed tone as if she had other things to do.

"Hello, Mrs. Garcia," I replied in unison with Kiara and Amelia.

"We have a question about the talent show," Amelia said nervously while fidgeting with her hands. There is quiet in the eye of the hurricane, I randomly thought. Quiet and then tragedy. Were we in the eye of a hurricane? Were we even in a hurricane? Was I just being dramatic? I knew one thing for sure – the waiting was killing me.

"We are the kids that got in trouble for making the yellow banner." Mrs. Garcia looked us over as if searching for hidden weapons. "Our punishment included no participation in the talent show so we weren't able to attend the elimination rounds that were held this morning," Kiara said. She paused and took a deep breath, "however, we did not make the yellow banner, and the principal now knows this, so we *are* allowed to enter the talent show. We were wondering if there are two spots left over from the elimination rounds."

Mrs. Garcia looked at us with open sympathy. "Sorry girls," she said while sighing. My heart sank into my shoes. We wouldn't be able to be in the talent show.

Chapter 12

IT'S A BAND

I scolded myself for feeling so disappointed. After all, I had known this would most likely happen. "There is only one spot left," she continued. "You can decide amongst yourselves who is taking the spot, or you can send in videos and I'll pick who gets the spot." A phone rang in the distance. Mrs. Garcia perked up as if she had been waiting for the phone to ring all day. "Excuse me girls," she said before rushing off.

"You two can have the spot," Amelia said decidedly. "Diamond, I know how much you like playing the flute and how good you are. Kiara, I bet you're great at the saxophone. Anyways without you two talking to Max in the first place we wouldn't even be able to enter the talent show," she said looking very sad but seemed confident with her decision.

"I couldn't Amelia!" I exclaimed. "You deserve to be in the talent show. You sing better than most professionals, and I know you'll win first place."

"Yeah," Kiara agreed. "And this way we wouldn't have to compete against each other."

"I can't do that," Amelia said, crossing her arms across her chest. "If I accepted, I would regret it for the rest of my life. I just wouldn't feel comfortable knowing I stopped you from competing."

"Maybe, none of us should do it then," Kiara said. "Because I wouldn't feel comfortable taking the spot and I don't think Diamond would feel okay with it either. I mean all for one and one for all." We all high-fived.

The opposite of none is all, I randomly thought. I brushed the thought away, then I exclaimed, "Wait a minute!" Kiara and Amelia abruptly turned to me. "Why can't we all do it?"

"What do you mean? That's kind of the problem," Kiara said with her hand on her hip.

"I mean why don't we just combine and become a band!"

"That would work," Kiara said grinning.

"Yeah, that would be great!" Amelia said.

Right then Mrs. Garcia walked back in from her phone call. Whatever happened on the phone, she seemed extremely happy about it. "So, what's your choice girls?" she said, giving us her full attention for the first time since we've been in the room. She didn't even check her watch.

"We are all taking the spot. We decided to become a band," I said beaming.

"Good choice," Mrs. Garcia said as she started to shuffle her papers again. "I hope you do well in the talent show."

"Thank you," we said in unison.

"Now I'm going to ask you a few questions and put your answers into a form which I will then send to the principal. It's just a talent show band form," Mrs. Garcia explained. We nodded. "Okay," she said as she pulled out a form and a pen. "What are your names?"

"Amelia, Kiara and Diamond," I answered. Mrs. Garcia jotted down our names on the form.

"What grade are you in?" she asked.

"We're all in 7th grade," Kiara said. Mrs. Garcia jotted that down to.

"Okay. What do you want your stage name to be?" We looked at her as if she was speaking a different language. "You know... Your band name?"

"Oh um, I don't know," Amelia said shrugging. "Can we have a minute to discuss it?" Amelia asked sweetly. Mrs. Garcia nodded. We formed a huddle. "So, what do you guys want to be called?" Amelia asked.

"I don't know," I replied shrugging.

"I don't know either. How about 'Better Than Maggie'?" Kiara suggested. Me and Amelia broke out laughing earning us a suspicious glance from Mrs. Garcia.

"Um maybe 'The Flying Tigers'," I suggested.

Amelia snapped her fingers together and said, "I know! 'True harmony'! That would be super nice!"

Me and Kiara shrugged. To me the band name sounded okay but seeing the sparkle in Amelia's eyes I couldn't say no. "Okay, let's do it," I said.

"Yeah," Kiara agreed.

"Mrs. Garcia, our band name is 'True Harmony'," Amelia said smiling.

"That's a very nice name," Mrs. Garcia. Amelia began to beam. She smiled in thanks and then we walked out of her office. "Good luck in the talent show," she said smiling.

When we were out of the office Kiara laughed and said, "We definitely don't need any luck."

I smiled and replied, "yeah, we're going to blow Maggie out of the water."

"Even if we don't it'll just be fun to compete," Amelia added. As she said this, we heard the bus engines turn on from a nearby window facing the school parking lot. "Oh no, how long were we in the office?" Amelia said, panicking.

"Too long," Kiara replied. We all started running and burst out of the school door. We saw a bus pulling out and leaving along with hard, rapid rain.

"Oh, I hope that wasn't any of our buses!" Amelia moaned. Without planning it, we all shifted into a sprint. Kiara offered us a quick wave goodbye as she turned and ran into her bus. Unfortunately for me and Amelia, our bus was further down the bus line. The buses were leaving quickly, and the rain was pelting my face and eyes. I pulled my sweater closer to my body. Just as our bus was about to leave, we caught up to it.

The bus driver reluctantly opened the door and let us in. We walked in dripping water on the already wet and slippery bus floor. We found one of the only rows left and sat down. Even though I was wet and cold and out of breath, I couldn't suppress a grin. When I got home, I would get to tell my parents that I hadn't made the yellow banner and tell them about the video Max recorded. I leaned back deeper in my seat and smiled like a dummy.

Soon enough I was walking toward the door to my house. I timidly pushed open the door. My mom was standing there as if she was waiting for me. "Hello Diamond," she said. I was confused. Then I remembered that I was supposed to be punished. I better speak fast I thought.

"Hi mom," I replied as I shrugged off my sweater, rearranging my explanation of what happened in the principal's office in my head.

"I know what happened in the principal's office," my mom said teary eyed. "The principal emailed me. I am so sorry I didn't believe you." We hugged and I felt myself get teary-eyed too. My good name had been restored at school and at my house. I felt like I was on top of the world.

"It's okay Mom," I replied, and I rushed upstairs so I wouldn't cry. That day I got to pick where we went for dinner, and I had a great tennis practice. It felt so magnificent to not feel guilty. That night I fell asleep with a free consciousness, and I couldn't wish for anything more. Needless to say, I slept wonderfully that day.

Chapter 13

GROUP CHAT

The Next Day at Lunch

Amelia got back from the lunch line and sat down next to me with a smile on her face. "Yesterday after school was amazing," she said with a dreamy look on her face. "I'm not grounded anymore; I can freely talk to you again and I was treated like a queen by my family!"

"Yeah, yesterday was great!" I said, sighing. "I got to pick a restaurant for dinner and all the punishments were lifted. Everyone was super nice to me too." Then Amelia frowned while looking at me concerned. "What? Is there something on my face?" I asked, rubbing my hands over my face.

"Nope. Look behind you," Amelia said. I could hear the fight in her voice to stay polite. Honestly, I didn't even have to look around at that point. Only one person brought out that side of Amelia – Maggie. I turned to discover I was right.

Maggie was walking toward us like a girl on a mission. For some reason I couldn't turn away. I sensed something was wrong. She didn't... look perfect. Her hair wasn't perfectly brushed, her lip gloss wasn't evenly applied, and her boots even had a speck of dirt on them. She wasn't even wearing her usual confident sneer.

She took a seat at our table across from us. "You little horrible people!" She exclaimed as she threw up her hands in frustration. "Almost got me in trouble!"

I rolled my eyes and said, "Maggie, I really couldn't care less." Then the meaning of her sentence hit me. "Wait, what do you mean by almost?"

Her confident sneer returned. "Did you really think I was going to get in trouble? That's cute. All I had to do was sniffle, blow my nose a few times and said I had the good of the school at heart by putting an end to the yellow banner mystery," She laughed. "But anyway, that's not the point. I came here to say that I heard you guys and Kiara are entering the talent show as a band," She snorted. "Good luck! I advise you to back out if you don't want to be humiliated in front of the entire school. But I hope you don't back out. It'll be fun crushing you. As they say, the cream always rises to the top." I racked my mind for a good comeback. She got up and started to leave. "By the way, I'm the cream," she said grinning, as she sauntered away.

"You're definitely going to lose to us," I said, calling after her. All she did was laugh.

"What a mood killer," Amelia muttered.

"She really is," I said nodding in agreement. "Well, you know we just have to win now," I said just as I noticed two other people walking to our table. Was it "Bother Diamond and Amelia Day"?

I identified one of the people as Max. I guessed that the boy next to him was his friend. "Hello," Max said as he got to our table. I waved in response. "I'm really sorry about not showing the video to the principal as soon as I recorded it," he said.

"Yeah," the guy next to him said. "My name is Theodore. We heard that you guys were making a band."

"Yeah," Amelia said nodding.

"Well," Max said nervously as I began to drink my juice. "Can we join?" I nearly spit the juice out all over them. "We both overslept the day of the elimination rounds and we want to be in the talent show. We asked Mrs. Garcia if there were any spots left and she said you guys took the last one."

"Ummmmmmmm," I said glancing over at Amelia.

"Well, what do you play?" Amelia asked, taking a bite out of her muffin.

"Piano and keyboard," Theodore replied.

"Drums," Max said.

Flute, saxophone, keyboard, drums, plus a singer, I thought. That would either sound awesome or terrible.

"Well, how good are you?" I asked.

"I can play bumblebee on the piano and the keyboard," Theodore said. My eyes widened. Bumblebee is hard and super-fast. I'm light years away from playing that on my flute.

"I'm pretty good," Max replied.

"Well, I'll ask Kiara what she thinks," I said, contemplating their request. They walked away back to their table as quickly as they came.

"So... Amelia said.

"Do you think we should let them join?" Amelia asked.

"I don't know. I was looking forward to doing it with just you guys," I said as I took a sip of my juice.

"Yeah but it might be more fun, and sound even better with Max and Theodore," Amelia mused.

"Yeah, you know what, I think we should let them join." I decided.

"Yeah," Amelia concurred. "Keyboard, drums, flute, saxophone and a singer just might sound good."

I smiled, "Yeah! But let's do a phone call tonight with you, me, and Kiara so it's a group decision. Let's set up a group chat with Kiara in it." Amelia nodded.

"Sure," I agreed. "Thinking about Max and Theodore, I forgot about Maggie. What a jerk!"

"I can't believe she didn't get in trouble," Amelia muttered, sounding perplexed.

"Well, we'll beat her!" I said confidently. Amelia nodded smiling.

Then we began to eat our lunch uninterrupted. The silence sounded like music to my ears. Abruptly, a loud bell suddenly sounded, signaling that it was the end of lunch.

"Aww," I whined. "I didn't even get to finish my sandwich."

"And I didn't get to finish my muffin," Amelia added. "Well, I guess I'll eat it when I get home. See ya Diamond!" She said as she waved and hurried off to her next class.

"Bye!" I called back. I stuffed my food back into my lunch box and hurried to science class. In class, we learned about metamorphosis, and then in History we took a quiz, so I was more than happy when it was time to go home.

On the bus me and Amelia talked about the outrageously good episode of "Me and My Crazy Life" until we were at our bus stop. We waved goodbye to each other and went into our houses.

Once I was inside my house and had a more-than-moderate serving of Oreos, I flipped open my phone and began to text Kiara.

Diamond: Hey

Kiara: Hi

Diamond: Max and Theodore both want to join our band.

Kiara: What?

Diamond: Yeah. Theodore plays keyboard and Max plays drums.

Kiara: Do you think we should let them join?

Diamond: IDK. Me and Amelia wanted to do a group call so we could figure it out.

Kiara: That sounds good.

Diamond: Okay, I'll set the group call up.

I left our texting conversation and made a group chat with me, Kiara, and Amelia. Then I set up a group call with everybody. Almost immediately Kiara and Amelia joined the call.

"So, we all know why we're here today, right?" I asked formally.

"Yup," Kiara and Amelia said together.

"Okay then," I said nodding solemnly. "Let the case commence!

"Well, I think we should let them join," Amelia said. "Adding keyboard and drums could really make us sound like a professional band!"

"Yeah, but we don't even know if they're good," Kiara said.

"Theodore said he could play bumblebee," I said. Kiara murmured her approval. She has been trying to play "Flight of the Bumblebee" for a long time.

"Well, I still think we should just do it alone," Kiara said.

"Why?" I asked.

"I feel like it would be more fun with just us," Kiara responded.

"I think we should add them. I think it would make us sound really good and it might even be more fun," Amelia said.

"Well Diamond, what do you think?" Kiara asked me.

"I think we should...um...," I said deep in thought. Amelia and Kiara both had some good points. "Oh, I know. How about we let them try out. We'll judge how well they are at playing their instruments, and if they're nice, we'll let them join!"

"Okay," Amelia and Kiara agreed.

"Where would we do it though?" Kiara asked.

"I'll email the principal and ask her if she has space and time for us to hold tryouts," Amelia said.

"Okay," Kiara and I both said

Amelia quickly left the meeting to send an email to the principal. About 3 minutes later, she came back to the meeting grinning. "We can do it at 6:50 a.m. in the band room."

"Ughhh that's early," I said while sighing.

"Yeah, but it was the only time left. Apparently, everyone else has been practicing like crazy," Amelia said while shrugging.

"How are we supposed to tell Max and Theodore?" Kiara asked.

"I have Theodores number because we were doing a group project together," Amelia said. "I'll text him and explain the try out thing. I'll tell him to tell Max."

"Alright then. Well, this meeting is adjourned!" I said smiling. We all ended the call and left. For a full 5 minutes after that, I didn't do anything but fret about the talent show. I felt like we would lose badly to Maggie. I also imagined the humiliation I would face if I messed up in front of the whole school. If that happened, I would definitely have to switch schools. Too nervous to do homework, I went downstairs and played my flute. Playing the flute always calms me. The ability to make music and to learn how to play your favorite songs gives you power. Hearing the sweet high and low sounds filling the air and knowing that you are creating them gives you confidence. And working through a tough spot and eventually hearing your progress is so rewarding. It's like having an ice cream cone on a hot, summer day.

After my calming flute session, I forced myself to get through my homework, and then continued playing flute some more. I had dinner with my family and then I went to sleep. I dreamt that I was on a stage in this dream. Thousands of students were in front of me. In my hand was my flute. Strangely, Amelia, Kiara, Max, and Theodore weren't there with me. I was alone. I pulled the flute up to my lips and blew. A horrible, awful sounding melody erupted from my lips. I adjusted my embouchure, and I took deeper breaths before I played, but the noise wouldn't change. The crowd erupted in laughter. I brought the flute down from my lips and it hung by my side. I then willed myself to walk off the stage, but I couldn't move. I closed my eyes in shame. Then a sticky, slightly hard thing broke on my shoulder. I opened my eyes. I saw red. It was a tomato. Then thousands of tomatoes began erupting everywhere on me and I couldn't escape. I couldn't force myself to move.

It was then that Kiara rushed on the stage. Followed by Amelia, Theodore, and Max. Their instruments magically appeared on the stage as well. We began to play. I can't say if the music we played was good or horrible because I suddenly woke up. "My dreams are getting awfully vivid lately," I mumbled to myself. I glanced at the clock. "EEK," I shrieked as I saw the time. It was 6:40 and the school was 10 minutes away! I was going to be late for the try outs I was hosting! I put on my clothes and dashed to the bathroom to brush my teeth. Then, I sprinted downstairs, shrugged my backpack on my shoulder and grabbed my flute. It was 6:45, there was no way I was going to be on time for the bus. I grabbed an apple for my breakfast and took my lunch bag with me. I checked my watch again. It read 6:47. I groaned as I called upstairs, "Dad, can you drive me to school? I have an important meeting at 6:50."

My dad sauntered down the stairs, slowly as if he was on a Sunday stroll. Then he checked his watch. "Your meetings at 6:50? You're going to be late!" he said. He jogged down the rest of the stairs, slipped on a jacket and grabbed his car keys. I got my jacket on as well and pulled on my favorite tennis shoes. I quickly opened the door and stepped outside to discover that it was raining. No…it was pouring. But it was too late to go back inside and grab a umbrella and some boots. I was already late enough as it was. I ran to my dad's car as the rain pounded on my face and drenched my hair. Some of the rain droplets squeezed their way into my shoes, making my feet feel cold and wet. My dad followed, quickly unlocking the car as we jumped in.

"So, why is this meeting so important?" My dad asked as he drove to school.

"It's a try out for a band that me, Amelia and Kiara are making. It's for the talent show," I said as my hair slowly dripped water on my jeans. I groaned as we hit a red light.

"Cool," my dad said. I checked my watch again. It was 6:52. I was officially late. I placed my flute case onto my lap and took a bite out of my apple. 3 minutes later we arrived at the school.

"Thanks for the ride, dad," I said as I leapt out of the car, gathering my stuff.

"You're welcome," he said as he drove away.

I sprinted in the building and ran into the band room. My shoes squeaked with every step and my hair was dripping water on the floor as I burst into the band room. I surveyed the room. Max, Theodore, Amelia, and Kiara were already there. I was the last one to get there. I dropped my backpack on the floor and sped-walked over to the area they were practicing in. The air was already filled with music, and I don't think they had noticed me yet. Amelia was warming up her voice, and everyone else was doing scales. Even warming up, they sounded wonderful. I just stood still and listened, as the scales and singing settled in the air. I closed my eyes, evaluating how Max and Theodore sounded with Kiara and Amelia when I was interrupted in my thoughts.

"Oh, hi Diamond," Amelia said smiling. The music abruptly stopped.

"Hi," Kiara, Theodore and Max said.

"You're late," Kiara said with humor in her eyes.

"I have a good excuse," I said, racking my brain for a good excuse. "I um… overslept," I finally managed to say. Everyone burst out laughing.

"Well, I really like your hair." Amelia said. "I see you're rocking the wet look."

I reached up to touch my drenched curls. They looked elongated and shiny because of the rain. "Thanks," I said. "Although, I wasn't planning it." Amelia and Kiara nodded understandingly. I then sat down to unpack my flute and I quickly ran through a few scales as everyone did their separate warmups as well. When we were all well warmed up, I clapped my hands with a smile and said, "Let the auditions begin!"

Chapter 14

THE TALENT SHOW

Everyone stood up and adjusted their music stands accordingly. "So, Theodore, you said you could play "Flight of the Bumblebee", right?" Theodore nodded. "Can I hear it?" Kiara asked. She sounded slightly skeptical. As soon as the words left her mouth, Theodore's hands were flying over his keyboard. He didn't miss a note and he hit every key with such precision and skill it took my breath away. I felt my jaw drop. He played "Flight of the Bumblebee" better than most adults! When he finished, he just smiled as if he did that type of stuff every day.

"Wow, that was really good!" Amelia said grinning.

"Yeah," I added.

Kiara stood still for a minute. I felt the room grow colder as we waited for her verdict. "That was pretty good," Kiara finally said. I heard Theodore let out a breath. He didn't know it, but she was being typical Kiara. She may seem a little cold and distant when she doesn't really know you but as soon as you become friends the gooey side of her gushes out.

"So, Max what can you play?" Amelia said grinning.

"I made this up myself," Max said right before he delivered an excellent performance filled with cymbals, drums and perfect timing. When he finished, I was surprised my jaw didn't hit the floor.

"That was really good!" Amelia exclaimed beaming.

"Yeah," I agreed in awe. "But can you give us a moment for us to talk about your performances?" Max and Theodore nodded politely. Me, Kiara, and Amelia walked a few steps away and formed a huddle.

"They're super good," Amelia said. "We should definitely let them join."

I nodded in agreement "Yeah, they definitely have a really good mastery over their instruments," I said. "Like, their individual talents are off the charts! If we could weld all of our sounds together…," I did the mind blown expression with my hands.

"They *are* really good," Kiara admitted. Then she took me by surprise when she said, "So I think they should join."

"You do?" Me and Amelia asked at the same time.

"Yeah," Kiara said laughing at our shocked expression. 'I really think we could win or at least be really good if they join."

I nodded and with that we broke the huddle to go back to Max and Theodore, who both looked visibly nervous.

When Amelia stepped forward beaming and said, "Congratulations! You guys made the band!" They high fived each other and grinned like they had won the lottery.

When they were done celebrating, Max asked, "So what are we playing for the talent show?"

"Me and Kiara were thinking about doing Against All Odds," I said as I logged into my phone and played the song.

"I love this song!" Amelia gushed as she nodded her head up and down to the beat.

"Me too," Theodore said. We took a moment to listen to what we were going to play. When the song finished, we were silent for a minute.

Then Max broke the silence. "That sounds like it's going to be super hard though," he said. Everyone nodded.

"But, if we play it right it can be super cool," Kiara countered.

"Go big or go home," Theodore added.

"I'm sure we could learn it," Amelia said confidently.

"Yeah," I added.

Max didn't say anything. He just stood deep in thought for a minute. Then he said, "Okay! Let's try it!"

Kiara passed everybody the sheet music for the song . Then she gave Amelia a sheet of the lyrics printed out on it.

Everybody was silent as they studied their stuff. As I looked over my sheet music, I noticed a lot of high notes and impossible fast finger flying tempos sprinkled throughout the song. All in all, it would be the hardest song I ever attempted to play. Ever. I gulped. I didn't want to make a fool out of myself in front of my friends. I looked around and everybody else looked worried too. That made me feel slightly better. I instantly felt horrible that it made me feel better. But it also made me worried. Were we all in over our heads?

"Well, I guess we should try it," Theodore said his voice cracking. He was also nervous, and he could play "Flight of the Bumblebee". What were we attempting? We all nodded.

"Okay then. No time like the present. I guess I'll start us off." He raised his drumsticks over his head and cracked them together as he said, "One, two, three!"

Before I attempt to explain how we sound, I have to ask you a question. Have you ever been to a children's concert? You know, in elementary school where the kids are just learning their instrument. If you haven't been to one, their music sounds horrendous. Absolutely terrible. The squeaks and the unbalance and the lack of harmony would drive a musician crazy. That's kind of what we sounded like.

That said, you could hear the mastery over our instruments and Amelia's voice. Sure, there was the occasional squeak and the occasional missed note but overall, *as individuals*, we didn't sound too bad. As a group, however, we stank like month-old cheese. There was absolutely no balance. Everybody was competing for sound. Everyone wanted to sound like the star. This resulted in an overly loud unbalanced mess. My ears felt like they were bleeding. I could barely hear myself play. Thankfully the song finally ended. We stared at each other ashamed of the music we had created. So much for our band name, "True Harmony."

I decided to address the problem. I sighed and placed my flute on my lap as I said, "That stunk." Everybody nodded in agreement.

"Like smelly socks, dipped in vomit," Kiara added.

"There was no balance at all," Max said.

Kiara turned on him and said, "Yeah, because you were playing as loud as you could on your drums."

"Me?!" Max said looking offended. "You were playing as loud as you could on your sax. You completely ruined the song!"

"Guys!" Amelia exclaimed, annoyed. "This is exactly the reason why we're not in balance!" Everyone just stared at her Amelia took a deep breath and continued. "How can we be in balance in music when we have absolutely no balance as people?" She sat down and said, "Everybody sit down in a circle." We all groaned but we listened and sat down in a circle. We knew Amelia meant business. "We're going to play a game."

More groaning ensued. Amelia went on unfazed. She reached into her backpack and pulled out a little ball. "We are going to pass this ball around the circle. When you pass it to someone, they have to say why they started singing or playing an instrument." She smiled proudly and said, "I'll start."

She clutched the ball and took a deep breath. "I started singing to combat my shyness. My shyness was extremely bad. It got to the point where I couldn't give a class presentation. So, I learned how to sing in the hope that it would go away." She paused to beam proudly. "And it did. After you sing in front of a lot of people many times, it makes you feel like class presentations are the easiest thing in the world." She smiled and passed the ball to her right to Kiara. I sat in awe as I thought about what Amelia said. I was her friend for years and I hadn't even known that! I started to worry about what I would say. Why had I started the flute?

I was interrupted in my thoughts as Kiara said, "Wow, Amelia that's really cool." Amelia beamed. "The reason I started is not nearly as awesome as yours." She took a deep breath and said, "The reason I started the saxophone is really because I'm super competitive. I watched this 9-year-old girl play "Flight of the Bumblebee" perfectly on her saxophone. It sounded cool and I wanted to be better than her. I wanted to screech out high notes with ease and play faster than the speed of light. So, I started to play the saxophone."

Even though I already knew why Kiara started the saxophone, hearing the passion in her voice left me speechless. Kiara passed me the ball. I immediately started to panic. Why had I started the flute? I didn't really know. I felt my hands get sweaty as I felt the stares of the group. I took a deep breath and decided to find the answer as I talked. "I started the flute because I like music." Lame, I thought, cringing about the sentence I just said. I took a deep breath and tried to center my thoughts. "I decided to learn the flute at first because it was shiny and looked pretty. But I kept on learning the flute because I like the feeling of recreating my favorite songs and the satisfaction I feel when I perfect a rough spot. It makes me feel…" I paused looking for the right words, "calm and in control." As soon as I said it, I knew it was the truth. I passed the ball to Theodore.

"I'm not really great at school or sports. You know just average. I absolutely hate the feeling of being average. So, for like a year I was trying anything and everything in an attempt to find something I'm really good at. During that time, I learned I can't draw, play soccer or whistle, as well as a bunch of other stuff. After trying almost everything, I turned to piano and I found out I was good at that. Not just good, *really* good. So ever since I've been working to be the best at piano and keyboard," he said smiling and passed the ball to Max.

"Wow, okay, umm. After what you guys just said this is going to sound super shallow. I started to play the drums because my mom said I had to play an instrument," Max said smiling nervously. Everybody laughed and Max laughed too. "But now I really like it and I'm glad my mom made me learn it." He rolled the ball back over to Amelia.

Everybody stood up thinking about what we had said. I felt like I really knew Max, Theodore, Kiara, and Amelia on a whole new level. I think everyone else felt it too. In an attempt to lighten the mood, I said, "Well I'm thirsty and school starts in five minutes. Let's get water."

Everyone nodded and walked out the door to the water fountain. On our way there, Kiara paused in the middle of the hallway and said, "Do you hear that?" Everyone stopped and strained their ears for a sound. I could barely hear the faint sound of music. But even though it was soft, you could tell it was awesome.

As if we had planned it, we crept toward the sound until we found the door where the music was coming from. In short, the music sounded wonderful. The only thing that was not great about it was the harmony. The singer was obviously the star of the band. I mean the singer sounded amazing, but she wasn't blending in with the rest of the band well because it sounded like she was trying to stand out. Nevertheless, every note was hit perfectly and the song made you want to dance along. "Who are they? They sound awesome!" I said.

"I don't know," Theodore said.

"Well, let's find out!" Kiara exclaimed. We shuffled to the door and peered in the window. Since I was in the back of the group I couldn't see through the window.

"Ughh," Kiara said annoyed.

"Them," Max sighed.

"Who is it?" I exclaimed annoyed. Everybody moved so I could have a good look at the window. I peered in and saw… Maggie's band!" I groaned.

"With Maggie starring as singer," Max noted.

"They are super good," Theodore said, taking his turn to peer in the window.

"But their harmonies are not great," Amelia noted. "If we can get in harmony and nail our song we can win!" Everybody nodded. I believed we could win but we had our work cut out for us. As we watched and listened to Maggie's Band, the bell rang. Quick as lightning her band packed up and headed out the door before we could leave, catching us watching them.

"Were you spying on us?" A girl I didn't know asked as if we had committed some grand crime.

"Chill out Sophie," Maggie said, flipping her hair over her shoulder. "They just want to know what greatness sounds like."

A boy that I didn't know laughed as if that was the greatest joke in the world. "You want to know what greatness sounds like?" Kiara asked, crossing her arms over her chest. "Listen to our band practice. We are totally going to kick your butt at the talent show."

"As much as I'd like to take you up on your boring offer I have to decline. You know some of us have a life," Maggie said laughing.

"Maggie, I heard 2's your favorite number. Is it because your band sounds like you went number two?" I countered.

Sophie's mouth went into a surprised little O. "Insult us all you want. You and I both know who's going to win at the talent show. We heard your awful, pathetic, loud, excuse for a band practice from this room. It sounded like someone looking at your face for the first time!"

"You guys sound like you're constipated and saw your reflection for the first time," Kiara countered.

"Girl, bye!" Maggie exclaimed as she sauntered away out the door. The rest of her band hurried out the door after her.

"We have to beat her guys," Kiara said angrily. You could see the competitiveness and pride in her eyes. Oh boy, was Maggie in trouble now! Everyone nodded and then hurriedly split off to their separate ways to class as the warning bell rang.

The rest of the school day was horribly boring, and I was extremely grateful when it came to an end. Walking to the bus stop, I let my thoughts wander daydreaming about the talent show and I didn't even notice Kate walking beside me until she startled my thoughts as she said, "Hello." I noticed her voice still had an edge of cold, but it didn't sound like an ice bath in Antarctica anymore.

"What Maggie did was wrong. She shouldn't have framed you. She got you and your friends in a lot of trouble. You guys shouldn't have tried to record me either though. But I forgive you for it. I heard you're entering the talent show. Good luck," she said. As we boarded our bus she looked back at me, smiled and said, "You're not going to beat Maggie or I though." She was a part of Maggie's band? How had I not noticed?

I laughed and said, "We'll see!" Kate really is a cool person I thought as I boarded the bus. We could probably be good friends. But as soon as we got on, Maggie spotted Kate with me. Maggie gasped as if she witnessed a horrendous crime.

"Kate!" Maggie exclaimed, throwing her hand to her mouth. "What are you doing with her?!" Kate passed me an apologetic glance and went in the back of the bus to sit with Maggie.

I went to sit down next to Amelia thinking about the talent show and Kate when Amelia breathlessly said, "Have you heard?"

"Heard about what?" I asked absentmindedly.

"The big prize for the talent show!" Amelia gushed.

I immediately switched my full attention toward Amelia. "No. What is it?" I asked excitedly.

"Third place gets a third-place medal for the group and a 25$ gift card to an ice cream shop each. Second place gets a second-place medal and a cool coupon book for free slushies, pizza, and stuff like that each. And the first-place prize is super cool. The group or person that wins the talent show gets VIP front row seats to an NBA basketball game, a big shiny trophy and the chance to perform your act at the halftime performance!"

"Wow," I said amazed. "All the prizes are cool, but first place prize takes the cake!" I exclaimed, amazed.

"I know it would be so cool to see the NBA players up close if we win the talent show. I hear they're like 6 feet tall each! Plus, playing in front of all those people would be super cool!" Amelia gushed.

"First off you mean when we win the talent show," I corrected gently. We both started laughing.

The bus pulled up to our stop and we got off still laughing. We waved goodbye to each other and entered our houses. I got in my house, said hi to my mom and ran upstairs to my room, gently caressing my flute case. As soon as I got in my room, I unpacked my flute and proceeded to do some scales to warm up. Then I took out the sheet music for "Against All Odds". I took a deep breath and played through the song. There was one part in the song that switched from very low to very high quickly that I completely messed up on. My low C didn't come out most of the time and I completely bombed the fast part of the song, which is a quarter of the song. In short, I had a lot to work on.

I sighed and started to work on the fast part. I had to practice it at a quarter of the speed to start off. I decided to do it five times perfectly before I increased the speed. After my 10th humiliating time trying this and failing miserably, I flopped on my bed. Then I groaned a long, long groan. I grabbed my flute and walked over to my window. I opened my window and dangled my flute over the ground. It looked millions of miles away. I pictured it smashing into a million pieces. I wanted to drop it badly. I felt my finger loosen. Then I thought of the band's faces when I told them I dropped my flute out my window. I imagined my parents' faces. I closed the window and walked back to my desk. I sighed and began to play. I wasn't going to leave until I got it right.

Chapter 15

TRUE DEFEAT

"Wake up!" Someone yelled as a pillow hit my face. "Ughhhh leave me alone," I replied groggily.

"Get up," he shouted. That was Brayton's voice, I realized. I tentatively opened my eyes. "Hurry up and get ready or you're going to be late for your practice," he said annoyed. "Maybe you shouldn't stay up all night playing your flute and you would wake up on time for once," he added as he walked out of my room.

I frowned and abruptly sat up. Lying in front of me was my flute and my "Against All Odds" sheet music. I suddenly remembered my late-night practice session and checked my watch. I groaned as I saw the time. 2 minutes until practice started. I was even later than usual! But on the plus side I was sounding a lot better playing "Against All Odds". I hurriedly packed up my flute, grabbed my sheet music and slipped on my clothes. I ran downstairs where dad was already waiting for me downstairs with the car keys in his hand.

I smiled in gratitude, grabbed a granola bar for breakfast and then we raced out the door to the car. He drove me there faster than sonic and I ended up being only 3 minutes late. When we got to the school, I thanked him and raced inside to the band room to find the band warming up. They all looked kind of tired though. Even Amelia didn't look as enthusiastic as usual. I unpacked my flute and said, "You guys look tired."

"I am tired," Kiara replied. Everyone nodded in agreement. "You look tired," Kiara noted.

I nodded. "I stayed up all last night practicing."

"So did I," Kiara said.

"Me too," Amelia said.

"Same," Theodore said.

"Yeah, me too," Max said.

"Wow," I said. "Cool!" I said beaming. I was extremely lucky to have bandmates as committed as Kiara, Max, Amelia and Theodore!

"I want to know how much better we sound!" Amelia said beaming.

"Well, it won't be hard to sound better than yesterday's performance," Max said laughing. Everybody laughed partly because it was funny and partly because it was true.

I finished assembling my flute and ran through a few scales. Everyone else returned to their warmups too. When everyone finished warming up, we pulled out our sheet music and stood ready in front of it. Personally, I felt nervous and excited. I hoped we sounded more in harmony than last time.

"Okay," Kiara said. "So, I think we should run through it one time straight through and address the problems we come across afterward."

"Okay," everyone said.

Max raised his hands over his head and cracked them over his head as he said, "One, two three!" We played through the song and this time it didn't sound like a children's concert anymore. But it also didn't sound like 1st place material in the talent show either. There was still the technical mistake here and there from every one of us. It would take everyday practice from each one of us to nail this song. The harmony still wasn't great either. It was a lot better than yesterdays, but it didn't blend together as well as I knew we could. I didn't know how we could make it better.

I feel like everyone else was thinking the same thing, but no one had any ideas on how to make the harmony better either. So, Amelia awkwardly cleared her throat and said "We'll we could work on the last eight measures. Everyone messed up on that part." We all nodded and played through the part again.

The rest of the practice went like that. We just played through the parts we needed to brush up on and avoided the harmony issue because no one knew how to fix it. About 10 minutes left in the practice we had no idea on what to work on anymore. We were all thinking about what to do to make use of the last 10 minutes when I realized we hadn't told Mrs. Garcia that Max and Theodore joined the band. "Guys," I said, "Since Max and Theodore are a part of the band now, we have to tell Mrs. Garcia."

"Oh yeah," Kiara said. "I forgot about that."

"Let's tell her now," Theodore suggested.

"Okay," we all agreed.

We packed up our instruments and walked over to Mrs. Garcia's office. When we entered, it was evident that Mrs. Garcia was as busy, if not, *busier*, than our last meeting. She was on a phone call when we walked in so we had to awkwardly wait for her to finish the conversation. Her conversation on the phone went something like, "I'm sorry but our school doesn't offer a second change of pants." A loud angry blast from the other side erupted in Mrs. Garcia's ear. Even though the person on the other end was talking loudly I couldn't catch what they said. Whatever he or she said though it made Mrs. Garcia pretty angry. She tapped her fingernails on her desk and retaliated with "Ma'am we are not responsible to provide any students with a change of clothes. I am truly sorry your son's pants are drenched with paint but there is nothing I can do about it. He'll have to wear his gym pants or borrow gym pants from the PE teacher."

Another angry blast came from the other end of the phone. Mrs. Garcia sighed and said "Ma'am…" but stopped as she heard a click on the other end. The other woman had hung up. Mrs. Garcia sighed, hung up as well and muttered something as she rearranged papers on her desk. She didn't know we were in the room yet. I cleared my throat so she could know we were there. "Hello, children" Mrs. Garcia said as she looked up at us. Seeing her face fully you could see the bags under her eyes. She looked tired.

"Mrs. Garcia, if you're busy we can come back another time," Amelia offered.

Mrs. Garcia chuckled and said, "That's really sweet but you can stay." She put down some papers. "So, what do you need?" She asked.

"We would like to have Max and Theodore join our band," Kiara said.

At this, Mrs. Garcia put her hand on her chest as if Kiara had cursed. "I'm sorry children but that can't happen. I already submitted your form for the talent show to the principal. Changing it now, I would have to get the form from the principal, change it, and then submit it back to her. Then, everyone else will ask me to change their forms they already submitted because I changed yours." She looked off into space as if she was thinking about what would happen. Judging by her face it wouldn't be pretty. "I'm sorry, Theodore and Max won't be able to join your band." Mrs. Garcia said. She started to arrange papers on her desk again. I looked back to Theodore and Max. They looked like they had been smacked in the face.

"Mrs. Garcia," I said almost without thinking. "If Max and Theodore can't be in the band, can I withdraw from the band?"

She looked extremely shocked. "Well, you can just not show up for the talent show," Mrs. Garcia said.

"I would like to do that then," I said decidedly.

"Me too," Amelia said defiantly.

Kiara looked at me and Amelia like we were crazy. But then she smiled and said, "Me too" as well. Mrs. Garcia couldn't have looked more surprised if she tried.

"You don't' have to do that, guys," Theodore said.

"We know," Kiara said. "We wanted to."

"You should play," Max said, trying to reason with us.

"No, we shouldn't. It wouldn't be right," I said my arms folded across my chest.

There was silence from Max and Theodore. I almost forgot Mrs. Garcia was in the room when she said, "Are you sure? You know you don't have to make a decision now…" she added.

"We're absolutely positive," Amelia said and with that we left her office. I felt sorry for myself. After everything that happened, I wouldn't be able to play. But I didn't regret my decision. If I had to relive it, I would do the exact same thing and that's why I knew I made the right choice.

There was silence as we walked back to the band room. Loud, awkward silence. All you could hear was the thump, thump, thump, of feet. Not a word. "True Harmony" was over.

Chapter 16

TRUE HARMONY

In the band room I decided to break the silence. "Well, it was fun while it lasted," I offered. Silence glared back at me. I decided to stop talking. I sat down in a chair twiddling with my thumbs watching my watch tick the seconds off. I strained my ears for any sound at all. If you listened hard, you could barely hear Maggie's band. They sounded just as good as yesterday. More silence until Amelia's soft voice said, "Mrs. Garcia is tired and overworked." "Let's make her a card." Everyone nodded. It was so like Amelia to always think about other people.

We leapt into making the card. With a lot of cutting, drawing, and bedazzling, we quickly finished. We made the card in complete silence. I think that's what we all needed right then. "I'll give it to her," I offered. Everyone nodded and then we all signed our names on the card. One after another. As I signed. It I felt like I was signing my decision to not participate in the talent show in stone. I tucked it in my pocket and we sat in more silence. The bell rang, we gathered our stuff and left.

I walked out the band room and made the now familiar turn to Mrs. Garcia's office. My thoughts were swirling around in my head. I pictured Maggie's triumphant face when she'd find out we weren't playing in the talent show. I imagined her smug expression when she'd win and I knew she would win. I entered Mrs. Garcia's office. She was in another room making a phone call. I slipped in, placed the note on her desk and slipped out unnoticed.

I trudged through the rest of the school day half paying attention to my teachers. At the end of the day as I was passing Mrs. Garcia's office to walk toward my bus, I saw her holding the card me and my band had made. Our eyes met. For the first time I saw her she looked genuinely happy. I smiled and left to get on my bus.

Mrs. Garcia

Most children are rude and selfish. They only care about themselves and consider adults closer to aliens than as humans. But the little children that came in my office today – the very same ones that I crushed their dreams of being in the talent show – made me a card. Not just any card, the most splendid card I have received in my entire life. It nearly brought me to tears and one of them saw me as she was walking out the school. Her little face held no resentment. She just flashed me a smile well ahead of her years. Her smile seemed painful, but it was genuine. She was angry but she wasn't angry toward me.

That smile undid me. I immediately left my office as if I was on autopilot. I was on a course straight to the principal. I opened the principal's door, "Olivia," I said with great importance, "I need to change a talent show form."

Diamond

"Girl, you need to check your email," Kiara nearly screamed in our group video call.

"Yes. You need to check it!" Amelia said excitedly.

"Okay, I'll be right back on the call as soon as I check it," I said as I clicked off the group chat. I went to my email and clicked on my newest one. It was from Mrs. Garcia. I expected a thank you email for the card. Instead, what I read was completely unexpected. It said a change had been made in the talent show form I submitted. It said there is an addition to our band. It said Theodore and Max were going to be able to play with us! I put my hand to my chest and let out an excited shriek. We were back in the talent show!! I excitedly went back to the group video call.

"Did you guys get an email from Mrs. Garcia too?" I asked, pouring out my words in an excited jumble.

"Yup," Kiara said while smiling. "'True Harmony' is back on!" Amelia pumped her arm in the air beaming.

"I already texted Theodore that band practice is back on for tomorrow," Amelia added. "Speaking about band practice, I should probably practice my singing and I have homework. Bye guys!" she clicked off the video.

"Same here bye Kiara," I said.

"Bye," Kiara replied. Then we clicked off the group chat. I excitedly went to my desk and broke out my flute. I had a lot of practice ahead of me.

The Next Day

I arrived in the band room late as usual equipped with my flute in hand. I was greeted with smiles from my bandmates. "I can't believe Mrs. Garcia changed the talent show form. She put more work on herself to make us happy. That was nice of her," Theodore said.

"I'm just really glad she did it," Kiara said.

"Were you guys really going to miss out on the talent show if we weren't able to play?" Max asked.

"Yeah," I replied. "We weren't lying," I said, feeling offended.

"Wow, well that's really nice of you guys" Max said. I smiled and unpacked my flute. I ran through a few scales while everybody else did their separate warmups. There was a slight tension in the air. No, not tension. It was finally the feeling of mutual respect. I felt connected to everybody in the band room for the first time. Not just Kiara and Amelia, but Max and Theodore too. Everybody finished their warmups and pulled out their sheet music, including me.

"Okay. I'll count us off," Max said. He raised his drumsticks over his head. "One, two, three!" He said as he cracked his drumsticks over his head. This time, while we played, it didn't sound bad. There were still the technical mistakes from every one of us that wouldn't go away without intense daily practice. But it sounded in harmony for the first time. It was on the tip of perfection. When we finished, we looked at each other with proud smiles on our faces.

Then Amelia said, "We finally blended." That was all we needed to hear. Everyone started whooping and cheering, forgetting completely about the technical mistakes we had committed. We finally blended.

Chapter 17

GAME TIME

"Okay guys these are the last minutes of our last band practice. Today is the talent show!" Kiara declared, pacing up and down in front of our little group. Me, Amelia, Max and Theodore were all sitting on the floor patiently listening to her little speech. "We finally smoothed out the technical mistakes and our harmony is on point. All we can do now is relax and wait," Kiara said. "Plus, there's only five minutes left. So, rest up today and come back at 5 ready to kick butt in the talent show!"

"Oh, yeah!" Everyone cheered. We placed our hands together and chanted, "True Harmony!" Then we packed up our instruments and sat together waiting for the bell. I don't know about everyone else, but I felt like a nervous wreck. I clutched my flute closer to my chest. The bell rang and we exited the band room. Maggie and her band were walking in the hallway right next to the band room and the bell only rang about 30 seconds ago!

Maggie and her band gave us the entire stare down package. My band returned the favor. Maggie flipped her hair and simply said, "Good luck at the talent show. You're going to need it," and walked away. Why did I think she was right and why hadn't I seen Kiara with the rest of the band? Anyways needless to say the rest of the school day I was a wreck. I wished the clock to speed up so the talent show could finally come but I also wished it would slow down so I wouldn't have to go at all. I threw up three times.

In my house, waiting for the talent show I tried to keep all thoughts away from it. I failed miserably. I checked my watch. It said I had 2 hours until I had to perform for the talent show. Sometimes waiting is the worst part of something. I flirted with the idea of playing through "Against All Odds" again but I realized there would be no point. At this point I either knew it or I didn't. I decided to do my hair in advance, so I wasn't rushing last minute because I'm quite good at that. I went downstairs to look for a brush. Downstairs in the kitchen were Mom and Dad.

"Are you ready for the talent show?" My dad asked.

"Yeah," I replied, smiling looking in the hair supplies bin for a brush.

"Are you nervous?" My mom asked.

141

"A little," I replied, grabbing the brush from the bin. That was a humongous lie. I don't think I have ever felt more nervous in my life.

"You shouldn't be. I know you're going to crush it," My dad said.

"Thanks dad," I replied heading upstairs. That comment made me feel better. I felt less nervous and calmer.

"Oh, Diamond," My Mom called after me. "Grandma and Grandpa texted me. They said they're coming to the talent show and they can't wait."

"Really?" I said, trying to keep the fear out of my voice. "That's great," I replied as I hurried upstairs. My anxiety rose from 50 to 100. Don't get me wrong. I love my grandma and grandpa. It's just that I don't want to mess up in front of them. But if I did a good job everyone would be so proud. It would make all the mess I had to put up with and all those long hours of practicing worth it. I let my thoughts wonder as I brushed my hair up into a bun.

Then I went into my bedroom and ravaged my room for an outfit good enough for the talent show. I tried on nearly every outfit in my closet, but I couldn't find anything perfect for the talent show. "To fancy," I muttered as I threw a dress to the side. "Too tight," I muttered as I threw a pair of jeans across the room. "Too dirty," I said as I threw a white shirt (now brown) across the room.

"What are you doing Diamond?" Diana asked followed by Deliah.

"Trying to pick out an outfit for the talent show," I replied, throwing another outfit across the room.

"What about this one?" Deliah asked.

I prepared myself for a lot of whining when I told her I wasn't going to wear it. "Deliah," I said as I turned and faced her. "That's perfect!" I exclaimed as I took it from her. It's a red jumpsuit with pretty, white flowers decorated on it. It was the perfect combination of chic and effortless beauty.

"I'm bored Deliah. Let's go outside and play soccer," Diana said. Delia nodded and they walked out of my room as I tried on my jumpsuit. It was absolutely perfect. Now as Kiara had said earlier all I had to do was wait.

5:00 p.m.

"Oh my gosh, oh my gosh, oh my gosh, oh my gosh, oh my gosh," I murmured repeating the words trying to find some sort of calm. The first act was scheduled to start in 30 minutes. We are the 5th act. Maggie's band is the first. Amelia was starting to look pale. Kiara was clutching her saxophone for dear life and Max was clutching his drumstick. Theodore was sitting in a corner in front of the trash can trying not to throw up. Of course, this was the moment Maggie and her band decided to come in and rehearse.

"Oh my goodness," Maggie exclaimed. "I have never seen a sorrier sight in my life. It's going to be easier to win than I thought" Laughter followed her statement. I was too distracted in my own head to retaliate. Even Kiara didn't have a clever retort. Maggie and her band strutted away to the other side of the room.

"Wait," I said, struggling to form words. "Where's Kate? Isn't she a part of your band?"

"No, who told you that?" A boy behind Maggie asked. Then they continued to walk away. I pondered what the boy had said but I pushed it out of my mind as the anger I was feeling toward Maggie grew. But I looked around and I knew she was right. There was no way we were going to win the talent show... like this.

"Guys," I said standing in front of my band. "As much as I hate to say it, Maggie's right. We have got to get it together. We are a great band and there's no reason to be scared," I said remembering what my cad had said. "But now that we know Maggie was right. Let's make her wrong," I said, knowing how cringey I sounded. Theodore moved away from the trash can to join us. Amelia and Max let go of their death grips on their instruments. Amelia gradually began to look like her regular self again.

"You're right," Kiara said, snapping back to her regular self. "Thanks for that Diamond," she rubbed her hands together grinning. "Now, let's rehearse so we're actually ready when it's our turn to get up there and kill it!" Everyone nodded. We unpacked our instruments, ran through scales, warmed up voices, and rehearsed the song. All in all, I don't know how we could possibly sound better. We were harmonized, our notes were clear and the music was a hit in the right pattern. We couldn't have been more ready.

I couldn't have felt more nervous. Forget butterflies in stomachs. I had full on lions, tigers and bears fighting a war in there! Watching the audience trickle in until almost every seat was filled and seeing everyone I cared about in the audience was beyond nerve racking.

The thirty minutes flew by faster than the speed of light. Way before I was mentally prepared, the principal was on the talent show stage, giving the annual speech. But I couldn't hear a word. I was too busy being nervous. If Maggie's Band was nervous, they didn't show it. They couldn't have looked more relaxed if they were on a beach drinking smoothies. Suddenly, the principal said, "Welcome Maggie's Band!!" The crowd cheered as Maggie and her band rushed on the stage. They sounded wonderful. They were going to be hard to beat. The only thing off about them was their harmony. It sounded slightly off. Not horrible, but not blended either. However, every note was nailed and every note clear as a bell. Maggie as a singer was especially good too. You could tell she was the star of the band.

The crowd was absolutely loving it. The claps were so thunderous and the cheering so loud I thought there was an earthquake. At the end of the performance two people started frantically throwing roses on the stage. I think they were Maggie's parents because they had the same exact hair and similar facial expressions as her. Regardless, whoever they were, they certainly liked the performance because they threw about 20 roses on the stage, which just encouraged the audience to cheer and clap louder. Most people even started standing up. The judges were grinning like they won the lottery. Maggie's band left carrying tons of roses and a smug expression. "Beat that," Chloe said grinning proudly.

"Don't worry. We will," Kiara said as they went to pack up their instruments. Then we turned our attention back to the talent show to scout the rest of our competition. The next act was a lot less impressive. It was a group of three and they were dancing to a fast-paced song. They probably should've picked a slower song. They couldn't stay on beat because the beat was too fast. Then, I think someone forgot their choreography because they just froze in the middle of the song and wouldn't move. At the end of the song, they left the stage to polite clapping. They looked crazy embarrassed. I started to worry again. What if I froze? What if I messed up during the fast part of the song?

"Excuse me guys," I said to my band as I went to the trash can feeling like I was about to throw up. On my way over there I saw Kate. "Hey Kate," I said, rubbing my stomach trying not to throw up.

"What's up Diamond?" Kate replied. She placed a large black hat on her head.

"Are you in the talent show?" I asked, growing confused. Only people competing in the talent show could be backstage.

"Yeah. I'm the fourth act." Kiara replied.

"Good luck," I said.

"Third act is almost done Kate. Are you ready?" A girl asked Kate. Probably her partner. She gave a huge plastic saw to Kate and started pushing two big, wheeled boxes toward the stage.

"Yeah," Kiara replied as she helped her push the boxes. "Bye Diamond," she said smiling as she picked up a long stick. I wondered what her act would be. Then I started to feel the entire zoo in my stomach again as I realized I was on after Kate. There was no time to throw up. I walked back to my band just as everyone started picking up their instruments and microphones. Amelia looked extremely nervous.

"This is a lot more people than I usually play in front of," Amelia said clutching her stomach. "I feel faint."

"You'll be fine Amelia," I promised.

"Yeah, you're the best singer here by far," Theodore added.

"Okay, does everyone have their stuff together?" Kiara asked. This was the first time I've ever seen her look nervous. My stomach began to churn again.

"Yeah," we all replied. I clutched my sheet music so hard it began to crumple. I decided to place it on my stand so I wouldn't tear it apart. I began to stroke my flute up and down. The cool metal calmed me just a little bit. Suddenly, loud and thunderous applause broke out within the crowd. Almost as one, me and the band leaned over to see what was happening. What I saw took my breath away. Kiara was standing over a girl in a box with a saw. With one clean swipe the girl split in two.

"Oh my, what a klutz I am," Kate exclaimed. "Well, I'll just have to put her back together again. Say it with me guys." The audience chanted with Kate, "abracadabra!" Kate pushed the boxes back together and the girl jumped out the box perfectly whole. The crowd cheered, cheered and cheered. My jaw dropped. Suddenly the girl that used to be in the box sneezed.

She went into her pocket and came out empty while saying, "Oh my, I'm out of tissues."

"Allow me," Kate said beaming. She took her hat off her head and tapped it upside down to show it was empty. "Hat, oh please prepare us tissues so Aleah's cough doesn't give us issues." She waved her magic wand around the hat for effect. Then she stuck her hand in and pulled out a box of tissues. The crowd went crazy. Kiara handed Aleah the tissue box. A little boy in the audience sneezed. Aleah threw the box of tissues to him. The little boy looked at the box of tissues as if it was gold. I looked at the judges. Their grins couldn't have been wider.

Me and my band turned away and looked at each other stunned. "Kate is really good," Amelia noted.

"You can say that again," I said. Another burst of applause and cheering ran through the audience.

"But, we can be better," Kiara said. "Let's go out there and play the best that we can. We can win. I know it. Come on True Harmony," she placed her hand in the middle of the huddle. Everyone else placed their hand on top of hers. "True Harmony!" we chanted. Then Kate and Amelia walked off the stage to more thunderous applause. I glance at the audience. They are all standing up. They got a standing ovation. The principal had to wait a long time for the audience to stop clapping so that she could talk.

After the audience died down Mrs. Jones cleared her throat. Then she said, "Please welcome True Harmony!"

I looked at my band and said, "Here goes nothing."

Chapter 18

WE DID IT!

I grabbed my stand, my flute, and my sheet music. I began to walk onstage. My feet felt like lead. The only thing that kept me going was my band mates behind me. I looked up into the crowd. Huge mistake. I saw my entire family grinning and snapping photos. My legs turned to jelly and suddenly I wasn't moving. I was a statue. Then I felt Kiara's hand on my shoulder. My legs started to move again. I heard Theodore's fast breaths behind me. I heard the big deep breaths Amelia uses when she tries to calm herself down. Somehow, I made it in the position I was supposed to be in. I placed my music stand on the ground and felt like I was moving in slow motion. I put my flute up to my mouth.

Everyone was in their positions by now. Theodore began to start us off, "One...," "I looked up into the crowd. I looked into my family's proud expectant faces. I couldn't let them down. "Two…," I looked behind me. I saw Maggie's smirking face from backstage. I remembered what I've gone through to get here. I couldn't back down now. "Three," I felt sick to my stomach – new kind of nervousness I had never felt before in my life. I took a deep breath and began to play.

Don't mess up, don't mess up, don't mess up, I chanted to myself in my head. I breezed through the first 10 measures. We sounded good. No, better than good. Great. But we were quickly approaching the fast part of the song. Out of nervousness, I bombed the next high note. I nearly died of embarrassment but I kept going. I let myself get lost in the music. I forgot about Maggie, I forgot about the crowd, and I forgot about the talent show. My notes began to come out crisper and cleaner. The band's harmony rose to a level we had never hit before. Everyone sounded crazy good. We were unstoppable. We breezed through the fast part as if it was pie. The rest of the song came out amazing and Amelia's voice sounded like she was a professional singer! Before I knew it, the song ended.

I closed my eyes, unsure what to expect from the crowd. I then heard whistles, and thunderous clapping. I opened my eyes. The audience was on their feet clapping and whistling as if their life depends on it. I looked at my family. They were absolutely ecstatic. "That's my girl," my dad belted out. The judges were grinning and I felt like I was flying. We began to collect our stuff and walked off the stage. When we are off the stage, we all let out proud shrieks.

"That standing ovation was crazy!" Kiara exclaimed.

"I know right!" I agreed.

"I wish I knew that would happen though. When we walked on the stage, I felt like I was going to throw up," Theodore said.

"Same here," Amelia said.

"Do you think we got first place?" Theodore asked. Everyone looked at Kiara.

"What are you looking at me for?" Kiara asked.

"Well, you're brutally honest and we need an honest opinion," Max replied.

"Humph!" Kiara said, faking anger. Then she switched to serious. "Guys, I really don't know. I know it's between us, Maggie's Band and Kate," she shrugged.

As we were talking, another act performed. This act was another band but not a very good one. They squeaked, were offbeat and they had okay harmony. We walked back to our little space backstage and packed up our instruments. As we were doing this, Maggie's Band approached. They all had their hands on their hips.

"You're not as bad as I thought but there is no way you're going to beat us," Maggie said confidently. "You might as well start your pity party now."

"Maggie, Maggie, Maggie," Kiara said. "We must have watched different performances out there because there is no way you saw what I saw if you think you won," Kiara shot back.

"Your performance was straight up trash," Chloe said rolling her neck. "You know we won."

"Excuse me!" I said annoyed. "You know perfectly well your performance couldn't match with us if we had our hands behind our back!"

"Oh, yeah! Well..."

"Guys!" Amelia said, throwing her hands up irritated. "Can't we just wait until the judges make their decision? There's no need to argue."

"Yeah," Theodore agreed.

"Finally, Amelia said something smart," Maggie said. Amelia looked infuriated but she just bit her lip.

I couldn't stand seeing Amelia angry. "Maggie, Amelia is probably the smartest person in the school. That insult didn't even make sense!" I protested.

Maggie didn't even acknowledge me. "The cream always rises to the top!"

"Is that the only thing you know how to say?" Kiara asked. Maggie and her band just sauntered away. Maggie is the only person that I know that excels at completely killing a mood. After that, everyone was in a sense of intense anticipation. We were all waiting for the talent show to be over and for the judges to announce the winner. We were also watching the talent show from backstage to see if anyone else was in competition for top three. In my opinion, no one else was. Before I knew it the last act was exiting the stage and the principal was giving a speech.

"Those were some wonderful performances out there, weren't there?" Mrs. Jones exclaimed. The crowd politely clapped. "I said, weren't there?" The crowd clapped louder and harder than I have ever heard anyone in my life clap before. "I agree. The talent on the stage was wonderful. Before we decide who won the talent show though I would like to say that this does not mean that anyone is bad at their talent. Everybody who performed today was absolutely amazing. I hope everyone who performed walks out of here with their heads held high!"

The audience cheered at that. As Mrs. Jones continued with her speech, Kate and Aleah walked over to our band. "You guys were really good!" Aleah said beaming.

"You guys were amazing too!" I exclaimed.

"Good luck!" Kate said, waving to walk over to Maggie's Band.

"I hope we don't need it," Max muttered.

"We won't," Kiara said confidently.

"Now please welcome the talent that made this talent show!" I walked onto the stage followed by my band and the other acts. The butterflies were officially back in my stomach. I snuck a peep at the judges. They were all wearing poker faces. I gulped. The crowd continued cheering. I glanced at my family. They wore excited, anxious faces. "Coming in a respectable third place," Mrs. Jones continued. She paused for effect. I wanted to strangle her. "Maggie's Band!"

"What!" Maggie shrieked. "How? We were robbed I tell you. Robbed! I demand a recount."

"If you can't handle this news, please exit the stage Maggie," Mrs. Jones said coolly. Maggie crossed her arms over her chest and sighed but she stopped complaining. "Please step forward to the judges table to collect your prize." Maggie and her band glumly walked up to the judges table, received their medal, and collected their ice cream coupon. I was filled with pride. Now, it was between us and Kate. Maggie and her band went to take their place in the audience.

"Now coming in second place," my heart lurched into my breath. I held my breath. She paused again for effect. "True Harmony!" Weirdly I didn't feel bad. We gave it our all out there and if that was second place it was second place. It is how it is. Anyway, at least we beat Maggie!

We walked over to the judges. "You guys were great," one of the judges said as he handed me my medal and coupon book. Me and my band went to sit in the audience.

"I'm not as disappointed as I thought I would be," Max noted.

"Yeah, it's because we did our absolute best and we had fun. I mean, winning's not everything at the end of the day," Theodore said.

"Yeah, plus, second place is still really good," I said flipping through my coupon book. "Hey guys we get a coupon for a free medium pizza!"

"Cool," Theodore said.

"Want to meet up there as a group after this?" Kiara asked.

"Sure," everyone agreed. We group high fived. "True Harmony," we chanted

"Coming in first place," Mrs. Jones continued. "The Magnificent Magicians!"

Kiara and Aleah let out a squeal. I genuinely felt happy for them. They deserved it.

Kiara and Aleah looked at each other then and then looked at us. They did that three times. I started to get confused. "Mrs. Jones," Kiara said. "Is it correct that whoever wins first place gets the chance to perform at an NBA halftime performance."

"That is correct! Congratulations!" Mrs. Jones said grinning.

"Well," Aleah said. "We would not like to do that." A gasp spread through the audience. My jaw dropped. Who wouldn't want that awesome prize?

"We both feel like it would be weird to do our magic tricks for a NBA halftime performance," Kiara continued. "But we don't want that excellent prize to go to waste." Out of the corner of my eye I saw Maggie tilting on the edge of her seat in expectation. "So can we give that part of the prize to True Harmony?"

"What?" Maggie exclaimed.

"Huh?" I exclaimed, my jaw dropping farther.

"Well, of course!" Mrs. Jones beaming. "True Harmony please get on the stage!" I felt like I was floating. I pinched myself hard. It wasn't a dream. I bounded on the stage with my band grinning ear from ear. Maggie was gaping like a fish out of water in the audience. "All of you, please collect your prizes."

I went once again to the judge's table. They gave me a piece of paper saying:

Congratulations! You are going to play in the October 2nd NBA Lakers Halftime Show!

Please contact 123- 466- 7789 for details.

Suddenly my family was next to me. I was surrounded in hugs, kisses, and well wishes. Maybe happy endings aren't bogus and maybe Maggie was right. Maybe the cream does always rise to the top. I can't contemplate that now though. I have a pizza party to go to with my band and my family!

The End

ABOUT THE AUTHOR

Ruth McGhee is a phenomenal teenage writer born and raised in Virginia where she lives with her four siblings, mom, and dad.

Diamond and the Talent Show, her first novel, is an attempt to showcase teenagers attempting to navigate life, lessons, and drama with a smile.

You can find her on Twitter and Instagram at
@RuthMcGhee.